Also by Josh Berk:

The Dark Days of Hamburger Halpin

JOSH BERK

GUY LANGMAN

CRIME

SCENE

PROCRASTINATOR

Alfred A. Knopf
New York

THIS IS A BORZOI BOOK PUBLISHED BY ALFRED A. KNOPF

Visit us on the Web! randomhouse.com/teens

Educators and librarians, for a variety of teaching tools, visit us at
randomhouse.com/teachers

Library of Congress Cataloging-in-Publication Data
Berk, Josh.
Guy Langman, crime scene procrastinator / Josh Berk. — 1st ed.
p. cm.
"A Borzoi book."
Summary: Sixteen-year-old Guy Langman, his best friend Anoop, and other members of the school Forensics Club investigate a break-in and a possible murder, which could be connected to the mysterious past of Guy's recently deceased father.
ISBN 978-0-375-85701-0 (trade) — ISBN 978-0-375-95701-7 (lib. bdg.) —
ISBN 978-0-375-89775-7 (ebook)
[1. Forensic sciences—Fiction. 2. Clubs—Fiction. 3. Fathers and sons—Fiction.
4. Death—Fiction. 5. Grief—Fiction. 6. New Jersey—Fiction. 7. Humorous stories.
8. Mystery and detective stories.] I. Title.
PZ7.B452295Guy 2012
[Fic]—dc23
2011023864

The text of this book is set in 11-point Goudy.

Printed in the United States of America
March 2012
10 9 8 7 6 5 4 3 2 1
First Edition

This book is dedicated to L. K. Madigan.

PART ONE

PROLOGUE

It's no coincidence that I got interested in forensics right around the time they put my dad in the ground. It was a beautiful day. Say what you will about the Jerz, but sometimes New Jersey can be absolute perfection. Mid-May, near the end of sophomore year. The birds were chirping a melodic song and the breeze was tiptoeing through the air—just enough force to kiss your face but far too polite to disrupt even a single hair on your head. According to the sign outside the First Bank of Berry Ridge on the way to the cemetery, the temperature was a lucky seventy-seven degrees. Those two lucky sevens stood crookedly, shining on in perfect symmetry. Seventy-seven degrees *is* perfection. The deep blue of the sky was perfect, and the wispy clouds looked like they sprang from a painter's brush. Everything was perfect. Yes, it would have been an absolutely ideal New Jersey spring day. If I hadn't been spending it at my father's funeral.

I had a bunch of tissues. Before we left the house, I jammed my suit pockets with them until my pockets were bulging cartoonishly, like I was a shoplifter swiping throw pillows. The last time I bought a suit was for my bar mitzvah, so it hardly fit. I looked ridiculous. I knew that. I had two whole boxes of tissues in there. I feared I'd need them all. I was wrong. I needed more. They only lasted a few minutes. All the tissues were sopping wet almost immediately, reduced to pointless mush. I ended up catching my

■|■

tears in my hands like a child collecting raindrops. Then I let them spill onto the grass. I knew there would be more. And more. And more.

It was my first funeral, but I knew what to expect. Somehow you just know. There were speeches that didn't mean much of anything. Pointless words of condolence. There was potato salad. Someone brought soup. There was that meaningless but gentle lie that "he's in a better place now." It's obviously stupid, because if it were true, if we went somewhere fantastic after we died, we would all try to hurry up and end our lives. But we do just the opposite. We fight like hell to stay alive. Dad fought. Tough old bastard. He lived longer than anyone thought he would. I plan to do the same. I had fun for a brief moment at that funeral, imagining myself and my friends as old men. What might we become? I pictured the foliage of my curly black hair gone, reduced to a gray ring like a line of shrubs around a suburban yard. I pictured Anoop walking with an old-man cane, wearing a toupee. I smiled. For just a second.

The service was distinctly nonreligious. The reading (which I gave, in a shaking voice) was not from any holy text, but from Walt Whitman, Dad's favorite:

> *What do you think has become of the young and*
> *   old men?*
> *And what do you think has become of the women*
> *   and children?*
> *They are alive and well somewhere;*
> *The smallest sprout shows there is really no*
> *   death;*

And if ever there was, it led forward life, and does
not wait at the end to arrest it,
And ceas'd the moment life appear'd.

Side note: Does replacing an "e" with an apostrophe automatically make something sound more poetic? *I lunch'd on school burritos; I fart'd for days.* Yup, sure is poetry . . . And sorry about that aside. Dr. Waters says I use humor as a way to hide my feelings. And since *I* don't have a psychology degree from Slippery Rock University, maybe we have to conclude that she is correct. Side note to the side note: Graduates of Slippery Rock University do *not* particularly enjoy it when you point at the diploma on their office wall and say, "That's not a real college, is it?" It totally is a real college.

The funeral went just like you'd imagine. There was the crawl of funeral-flag-bearing cars, winding like ants through the streets of Berry Ridge, NJ, to Dad's final resting place. I expected family to show up and I expected his old business partners to show up. I expected that his old shipmates would show up. I expected that, thanks to his long and colorful life, it would be a large and strange crowd. I expected that there would be some people I had never met.

But I didn't expect *quite* so many strangers. I thought a son would know most of the people at his father's funeral. I knew very few. Many I'd never seen before in my life. Like one guy—a tall, stooped stranger with a pale face and a dark blue flower in his black suit pocket. He looked like a number seven, bent severely at the waist like he was looking for something on the ground.

"Who *is* that?" I asked my mom through the tears. We were

outside now. The weather was lovely, people kept saying. Lovely. But outside was the worst part of the whole thing. The burial. My arms ached from carrying the casket. Pallbearer duties are normal for a son, I suppose, but you shouldn't have to do them in high school. I never thought I'd have to do them at all. Denial, I guess. Refusal to think about the future. Another way of hiding my feelings. Up yours, Dr. Waters.

The grass of the cemetery was the brightest green you've ever seen. It made me think of Whitman. *The smallest sprout shows there is really no death.* Death really is good for life.

"I have no idea who half these people are," Mom said. "I was going to ask you if you knew that fella." She pointed to another elder statesman. A guy who had to be Dad's age—something like seventy, anyway—with shocking white eyebrows. He raised them in our direction, that friendly funeral salute—lips pursed, head down, eyes solemn. Eyebrows. I expected Mr. Eyebrows to come over and talk to us, but he did not.

"And who is that?" I asked. This guy was younger—maybe Mom's age. I have a young mom. I'm the guy whose friends all like to tease him about how hot his mom is. Nice. But this guy wasn't good-looking. He was actually just *weird*-looking. He almost looked like he was in disguise. Maybe some people always look like they're in disguise. Maybe that's a good way to live. He had dark glasses and a magnificently bushy brown beard. He didn't even look at us, and he certainly didn't come say hello. He was anything but friendly. Mom returned the favor.

Others did come say hello, of course. Aunts and cousins, neighbors and friends. Anoop, my best friend from school, was there, as were his parents. Mr. and Mrs. Chattopadhyay greeted

Mom and me in that same sad way. Mr. Chattopadhyay's toupee was hilariously crooked, but no one said anything. Mom smiled a cheerless smile under her large dark hat. Her eyes were filling with tears again, so she extracted large-framed sunglasses from her purse and put them on. Like a body being lowered into the earth, her grief became hidden. Forever.

CHAPTER ONE

January. Eight Months Later. Forensics Squad, Day One

"Welcome to Forensics Squad!" The handwriting on the board is so chipper that it makes me snort. Who is that happy about forensics? Mr. Zant, apparently.

It is 2:45, fifteen minutes after the last bell. School is over, but Mr. Z's classroom is packed to the gills. That's a joke. Get it? Because Mr. Z's favorite subject is marine biology? But wait, I didn't already explain that, so there's no way you could have gotten the joke. Even then, it is quite possibly not funny. Never mind.

"Wow," Mr. Zant is saying, circling the room, handing out a form we all sign but don't read. He's very young, and he almost looks like a kid. "It is really cool to see so many of you," he says.

He *has* to mean that it's really cool to see so many good-looking girls show up for his club meeting. The hot girls are the main reason I joined up. Okay, I like the forensics shows on TV. And yeah, maybe I have sort of been one of those death-obsessed teenagers you hear about sometimes. Wearing a turtleneck, hanging out in cafés, reading books by Camus, stuff like that. (Not really. I hate turtlenecks.) But really, since Dad died last spring, I guess the idea of learning about how people die appeals to me. The difference between breathing and not breathing seems so thin . . .

Normally I don't love extracurricular anythings, and I didn't really want to join this club. But then Anoop told me that Mr. Z was hosting a weekly club starting after winter break that includes Laura Shaw, Aiden Altieri, Scarlett Reese, and Raquel Flores, and somehow I found myself penciling in my name on the Forensics Squad sign-up sheet. The last lass mentioned, the lovely Raquel, is of particular interest to me . . .

What can I say about Raquel Flores? Eyes like an angel, heart like an angel, and legs like an angel . . . Wait, do angels have nice legs? Do angels even *have* legs? I know they have wings, so they probably don't need legs. Forget it. I don't think Jews believe in angels, anyway. Just know this: There might be other girls who are a bit more popular, but there are none more beautiful or more mysterious than Raquel Flores. If she's not the sole reason I'm a member of Forensics Squad, her name on that list is certainly the factor that put me over the top. I'm crushing on her hard. I was interested in the topic, yeah, but still, it takes a lot to get me to sign up for anything. I'm not normally exactly what you'd call a "joiner."

Mr. Z continues. "It's just awesome that you are all into forensics. I should warn you, though," he says. "It's not at all like you see on TV. It's actually a lot of hard work, nitty-gritty science. We are going to learn the basics of crime scene investigation through a combination of lecture and lab, ending the semester with a simulated scene in the field. I will plant the evidence. You will solve the crime."

"Dude," I whisper to Anoop. "There are *four* ensics? What's an ensic, anyway? It sounds like something from health class."

"You're thinking of 'cervix,'" Anoop says, tapping his temple. "And there is but the glorious one."

"Your mother has four ensics," I say.

"Shut up your face about my mother," he hisses. "Or I'll kill you." He says "kill" like "keel" and motions with his finger like he's slitting a throat.

"And then I can figure out exactly how you did it!" I yell. When I think I'm funny, I have a problem with volume control. I slap the table. "Because I know all four ensics!"

The adorable Raquel Flores turns her head in my direction and narrows her dark eyes into a nasty squint. The look on her face lets me know that she is less amused and more confused. Story of my life. My mind goes to a piece of advice my dad gave me once. "Go where the pretty is," he always said. Worked for him. I've seen the pictures. He had some amazingly hot girlfriends before Mom. I cherish all of his advice. Live my life by it.

"What's all the commotion back there, Guy?" Mr. Zant says. Huh. I haven't been in any of his classes. We didn't take roll or anything. How does he know my name?

I wrinkle up my eyebrows and turn my head at a highly confused angle.

"What?" I say. "You must be some sort of genius detective." Smooth.

"Tell me your name, Guy," he repeats. Mr. Zant is one of those teachers who always try to be cool and hip and think of themselves as more of a friend than an enforcer, but I can tell he's getting sort of pissed at me.

"But you already know," I say.

"Dude," Anoop says to me in a low voice. "I don't think he really guessed your name." Anoop is good at figuring out social situations, unlike me. "Zant is probably one of those dudes who just call everybody 'guy.' He doesn't realize that your name is actually 'Guy.'"

"What are you whispering about, you guys?" Mr. Zant says, this time to Anoop.

"No," Anoop says, pointing both thumbs at himself. "Just one Guy. I'm Anoop Chattopadhyay. But you can call me the Bengal Tiger. Everybody does." Then he points to me with a double handgun gesture. "This goofy-looking Jew is Guy Langman."

Thanks, Anoop. He could have described me a million different ways. Noted my lovely curls, my naturally svelte build, my nose-of-much-character, my glowing smile. But no: it's "goofy-looking Jew." Could be worse, I guess. I smile weakly at Raquel.

Mr. Zant scratches his goatee and cocks his head.

I've never heard anyone, including Anoop, refer to him as "the Bengal Tiger." He's an Indian guy with hipster glasses and a valiantly-trying-to-be-a-mustache mustache. He dresses like a living Lands' End catalog. The Bengal Tiger? The whole room has turned tense, silent, and, if I'm not mistaken, a little angry. I stare everyone down and drum a quick rhythm on the table with my fingers.

"Don't get your ensics in a bunch," I say. "I'm here all week."

CHAPTER TWO

So, Forensics Squad. Do I go back? First meeting was hardly a success. I should turn and flee, really. My Flores chances, slim as they were, most likely were dashed by that outburst. I try to put it out of my mind. I coast through the week. Math, English, the click of the clock, the hum of school days. One Social Studies class *is* sort of interesting . . .

We are watching an "educational documentary" about a primitive tribe from an island somewhere in the Pacific Ocean. But no, that's not what is interesting. No one is learning anything here. Almost all the boys in class are just obsessed with snickering over the fact that in the movie, the topless tribeswomen's boobs are flopping around like pizza dough. The girls in class are all laughing about the strange dong bracelets that the men wear. Everyone laughs together when a shaman comes in to chase away evil spirits by biting everyone on the ass. He literally puts their cheek meat between his incisors and chomps down. Okay, this is interesting. Mostly just shocking. How did Mrs. Lewis *think* we were going to react? Did she fail to pre-screen this cultural epic? This is more uproarious than the time Mr. Brock kept talking about Honoré de Balzac in Lit class. (We all *swore* he was saying "ornery ball sack," and commenced laughing our asses off.)

But here's the thing: during the film, I find myself having deep thoughts about Dad. I find myself feeling profoundly jealous of the kids in the movie. The tribe's leader takes the boys—who are like twelve—and tells them *exactly* how to "turn into men." It is just so awesome. This leader, an extra tall, extra skinny wild man with eyes that move independently of one another, just sits these kids down, lights a pipe, and lays out the facts about what it means to be a man.

Some of it is fairly dubious stuff about how the world was cre-ated by a dragon who pooped fire or something, but most of it is a clear set of "rules for living." Stuff like how to shoot a pig with a bow and arrow, how to talk to women, how to be a husband, how to deal with disagreements with other men in the tribe. Although shooting a pig with a bow and arrow doesn't help that much in contemporary New Jersey. You see my point . . .

Anyway, I think: Why don't we have anything like this? Why don't we have a time when we sit down and learn the (narrator's voice) "rules for living"? We have bar mitzvahs, but all we learn there is how to sneak booze from an open bar. That may be *some* of the wisdom needed to be a man, now that I think of it, but still, I want a lot more. My rabbi isn't going to show us how to gut a pig (*treyf*), but the Torah portion I read at my bar mitzvah was liter-ally about cattle disease. No doubt this was useful back when the Torah was written, whenever *that* was, but it doesn't help me that much today. We need new rules, new traditions, new procedure manuals for life.

This is what I am thinking, scribbling in my notebook, sit-ting there in Social Studies, lost amid the thoughts of Dad, dong bracelets, pizza-dough boobs, and Raquel Flores's short skirt.

"You look like you're trying to solve the mysteries of life," Anoop whispers, in reference to the serious look I must have adopted while deep in thought. "Or maybe holding back a dump. Either way, let me know how it comes out."

I chuckle. And then I realize: My own dad, through all his little comments, all his quips, all his asides, *had* left me a kind of procedures manual. He had an amazing life—he was an inventor, a world traveler, a scuba diver who literally discovered sunken treasure. A mensch. He was always spouting gems. Pieced together in the right way, these gems might provide a road map through life's confusing wilderness. Now that he's dead, I can't get anything new from him, but maybe I can still get something . . . crucial. This thought hits me like a life preserver thrown to a drowning man, a floating inner tube in the raging sea that is my life. I know what I'm going to do: I'm going to write a book about my dead father. *Rules for Living* by Francis Langman, deceased. Maybe no one else in the world will ever read it, but maybe it will be just the thing I need to figure out how to live.

Then I join in laughing about the pizza-dough boobs and dong bracelets. They are pretty awesome. Can I say "dong bracelets" one more time?

Dong bracelets.

After Social Studies, Anoop and I go to lunch. School lunch sucks. Ever since the "healthy lunch" program began last year, there's no more pizza, burritos, barf-a-roni, tots o' tater, or even those awesomely gooey chocolate chip cookies. We can't even have peanut butter anymore, because one kid is allergic to peanuts and apparently can't be in the same room with even a dab of PB&J without having his face explode or something. That one kid happens to be the super-wealthy Hairston Danforth III. The Danforths donated a million dollars for the healthy lunch program, with the strings attached that it be peanut-free. There's no such thing as a free healthy lunch initiative.

Of course, various ingenious methods have been devised to sneak peanut butter into school, resulting in a whole thriving black market, much like the trade in stolen cell phones and prescription pills. And also, of course, now everyone calls Hairston "Peanut-Head." And, yes, they say it with a lisp on the "t" in "peanut" so it sounds like "Penis-Head." Mean, yes, but is that really so much worse than the name his parents gave him? Hairston? The only name worse than Guy at the whole school.

I am eating hempseed butter, which, no, doesn't get you high, and, yes, is disgusting.

"That looks like something that came out of my nose," Anoop says.

"Thanks," I say. It really is green and booger-ish.

"So, you staying after for Forensics today?" Anoop asks, chewing on some curried something he brought from home. He always packs. I tried packing my own lunch once, but found it too taxing. All that opening and unopening of jars, spreading things on things. My mom's not the "make your lunch" kind of mom. She's the "make it your darn self or take a five from my purse" type.

"I'm not so sure I'm going back," I say.

"Yesterday *was* humiliating," Anoop says. "But it really will look good on your college applications. And the ladies are still probably going to be in attendance."

"I'm beginning to think that chasing girls might be too much work," I say.

"Now, I know that you are a lazy bastard, Guy, but no one is too tired for girls."

"Meh," I say.

He throws down his fork. It's a plastic fork, which doesn't really make a satisfying clatter. Anoop doesn't let the soft plastic clatter slow him down, though. He's rolling. "That's what it's going to say on your tombstone," he yells. "Here lies Guy Langman. Meh."

"Well, yours is going to say 'Here lies Anoop Chattopadhyay: An Indian guy who became a doctor. Real goddamn original! ! ! ! ! ! !' Man, I feel bad for whoever has to carve that stone. 'Chattopadhyay' has a lot of letters. That would take 'em all day. Plus, I don't know if you could tell, but I said that with a lot of exclamation points at the end."

"I'm pretty sure they have machines to do that now."

"We can't even hand-carve tombstones for the dead anymore? What has happened to us as people?" I ask.

"*Some* of us are incredibly lazy bastards. But you really should come back to Forensics. You need something on your applications under 'Extracurriculars' besides video games, cartoons, and bubble baths."

"I'm learning useful skills playing video games," I say. It's not true. I spend most of my time playing an ancient Atari 2600 I bought on a whim. It came with, like, ten games for two dollars total, plus shipping. Obviously, a thirty-year-old video game system isn't for everyone, but it is pleasingly simple to me. The new video games are a workout. My favorite Atari game is Yars' Revenge. You get to be a bug or something, and it's pointless and thus perfect. A minimalist movement among video game players is going to come back. You mark my words.

"I'm working on a new project," I say, trying to derail Anoop. The book about my dad.

"That's cool and all, but . . . ," he says. He clearly doesn't believe me, even though it's actually true. "I can't believe you're not even *thinking* about college. You're smarter than ninety percent of these fancy-pantses who are applying to Ivy League schools."

"Fancy-pantses?" I say.

"Isn't that the plural of 'fancy-pants'?" Anoop says. "We brown people don't talk English no good."

Basically, every one of my classmates is certainly rich, and many of them are indeed headed for the fanciest-pantsyest colleges. But they are still putzes.

"What do you mean, *ninety* percent?" I say.

"Present company excluded," Anoop says.

"You ain't ten percent," I say. "Who else is supposedly smarter than me?"

Anoop starts counting on his long fingers. "Maureen Fields, TK, Hairston Danforth the Third."

This last addition to the list is a joke. Hairston is not at all stupid and is brilliant with computers, but he's hardly in the academic elite. More to the point, he's just . . . weird. "Poor, poor Penis-Head," I say, mainly just to change the subject.

"So, are you going back to Forensics or not?" Anoop asks. Changing the subject with him is like asking a bulldog to give up his bone.

"Anoop, I don't care about my college application, I don't really like science, and Mr. Zant's annoying," I say. All good reasons.

"Is there nothing that could change your mind?" Anoop says.

"Shut up," I say. "What are you so smug about?" He really *does* look smug. He's doing that thing with his chin that I call "the smug chin."

"Let's just say I have some information," he says, and takes out a piece of paper, folded in the intricate origami style that only girls can manage.

"What the hell is that?" I ask.

"But, Guy," he says. "You're *not* going to Forensics, so I see no reason why it should matter what—"

I grab for the paper and come up only with a fistful of air and a sleeveful of hempseed butter. "Damn you, Penis-Head!" I yell, mainly just as a joke, but Hairston looks over with a sad expression on his pasty face, and I feel a little stab that I added to what must have been the daily torture of life as Him the Third.

"I'll read it to you," Anoop says, unfurling the tiny paper with the sort of delicate motions that will one day no doubt make him a top surgeon. *"Anoop,"* he begins in a chirpy voice that speaks of money while still having a slight Spanish twang. *"Are you and Guy going to be coming back to Forensics? Yes or No. Circle one. From Raquel."*

I stop mid-chew, staring at him. Stunned. He hands me the note. It is as he described. Nothing too encouraging about that "from," but the "i" in "Forensics"—it is dotted with a little heart. A *little heart.* But wait—what's this?

"Her handwriting looks like your mom's," I say. Every day, up to and including this, our junior year, Anoop's mom puts a note into his lunch alongside the homemade curry. Every day I steal it and read it out loud. Take note that these, uh, notes, are distinctly not of the cutesy-lovey sort, but instead intend to convey things like "Don't forget the rules for solving the cosine!" Trigonometry tips in the lunch bag—classic Chattopadhyay. Anoop just shrugs.

I continue to stare at the note. Raquel Flores? Could it be? I can't think of a single reason why she would care if I would be at

Forensics Squad, except for the obvious one. Girls only ask this if they like you, right? Okay, I have dashing Semitic good looks, a sizable trust fund, and a charming personality, but I am hardly rich by Berry Ridge standards. Plus, there are dozens of guys cooler than me. Plus, her family is one of the richest of the local rich and she is seriously melt-your-face hot, upper-echelon popular.

And yes, let's get this out of the way: I go to Berry Ridge High School. And yes, it's known to one and all by the probably kinda obvious nickname "Very Rich High." (I won't tell you what they call Wyckoff High.) And yes, Berry Ridge *is* filled with a lot of rich kids. The *really* rich school nearby, however, is North Berry Ridge. Pretty much everyone just calls them "Stupid North Berry Ridge."

"Circle 'yes,'" I say, suddenly choking. My hempseed butter is turning to concrete in my throat. "Circle the beautiful 'yes.'"

CHAPTER THREE

So here I am, back in the dungeon. Mr. Zant's classroom is known as "the dungeon" because, well, the name fits. As a first-year teacher, Mr. Zant has one of the worst classrooms in the entire school. And the entire school is not exactly a high-gloss temple of modern learning. I mean, we have SMART Boards and laptop labs, but the bathrooms are crumbling and most of the windows are stuck shut. We're perpetually out of paper towels. And Mr. Z's room is dark and dreary, stuck in the basement of the school. Much of Berry Ridge High is actually half submerged, underground. There are small windows just below the ceiling, but otherwise you feel like you are indeed in a torture chamber well below ground. Rumor has it that the building was designed during the height of the Soviet Union Cold War paranoia. Apparently, back in the 1980s, the Russians, no doubt sensing the great strategic implications of our shopping malls and golf courses, seemed incredibly likely to point their nuclear warheads right at Berry Ridge. Having a bomb shelter for a school seemed a prudent and patriotic idea.

Mr. Zant's classroom is suspiciously less filled today. Most of the hot girls are gone. Most everyone is gone. Something fishy is going on. Get it? This time it makes sense! He specializes in marine biology! Fish jokes! But Mr. Z just smiles at the six of us who sit scattered around his otherwise empty classroom. Hairston is back, the weirdo. Then there's Anoop and me, in addition to the aforementioned nerds, Maureen Fields and TK. And what's this? Who else has returned? My, it's Raquel Flores for some reason. For *some* reason? Am I the reason? Or is she a secret intellectual? Smart *and* beautiful? Man, I think I love her. Are you supposed to talk to someone first before falling in love with them? Probably. I don't see it in the manual, though.

"I'm glad to see *some* of you aren't scared off by the idea of doing hard science," Mr. Zant says, calling our little group to order.

I *am* scared of "hard science" myself. I don't like "hard" anything—hard work, hard exercise, hard candy. Well, I guess I do sort of like hard candy. Who among us doesn't enjoy the occasional mint? But I prefer soft foods with less chewing. Soup, mashed potatoes, pudding—stuff like that.

I can't stop thinking, Why did Raquel come back? Does she really like me? She seems too pretty to like forensics. Maybe that's a stupid generalization. I don't like making generalizations. "People who make generalizations are idiots," my dad used to say. "Generally speaking." That's gotta go in the book.

The presence of the others makes more sense. What I know about Maureen is what everybody knows: that she was a total overachieving honor-roll-and-science-camp-type girl who recently underwent a Goth transformation that isn't fooling anyone. Over one long President's Day weekend she went away dressed in jeans and a cable-knit sweater and came back the following Tuesday in an all-black uniform featuring pants with about a thousand zippers and makeup that would easily gain her employment as an extra in a zombie movie (*Revenge of the Goth Nerds!*). She still seems sort of sunny a lot of the time, so it's just confusing. And her pants must take a really long time to get on in the morning . . .

TK—does he even have a real name? Everyone calls him TK. What can we say about him? Style-wise, first of all, he cuts his own hair. The result is fascinatingly uneven, and pretty much bald in spots. Anoop and I have theorized that TK probably invented some sort of electric scissors or robot barber that he is testing on himself. He also seems to bathe infrequently, and with little attention to detail. We have something of a metrosexual epidemic at Berry Ridge. Most dudes (besides me, the hard-core nerds, and a few choice others who keep it slackerish) are all model six-packy, primped and fancy. They always look like they just walked off a billboard trying to sell you a four-hundred-dollar pair of jeans. Not TK. TK dresses like he's about to punch his time card at an auto garage—full-on jumpsuits or grease-smeared jeans from the "stonewashed" age. He is also one of the prime peanut butter smugglers, having invented a variety of weird contraptions to sneak the banned legume into the caf.

Those eccentricities aside, TK does seem to be some sort of a genius, with skills in a variety of subjects. According to Anoop, who jealously tracks the other smart kids like a star athlete might check the stats on the opposing teams, TK is annoyingly well-rounded. He gets A-pluses in every class. In History he is able to wake from a class nap (TK is always tired) and instantly talk at length about the Sino-Japanese War of 1937. Who else even knows what "Sino" means? He is in AP Math, whizzed through Calc, and is also skilled in Gym and Shop class. He made a samurai sword out of wood! And he can run, jump, and throw with the best of the jocks. These latter qualities are what frosts Anoop's ass

the most. TK is like those guys on weird cable shows who have PhDs but also are good at building a bomb out of a toilet paper roll and preparing a crawfish soufflé.

I once asked TK why he was so tired. "Up late again," he said. "Doing what?" I asked.

"Research" was all he would say. Research into what? Ingenious peanut-smuggling devices? Robo-beauticians?

"Are you going to try to get Raquel to be your partner? You totally should," Anoop says.

I haven't been paying attention and didn't realize that Mr. Zant was assigning an exercise that requires a partner.

"That seems like a big step," I say. "I haven't actually even talked to her yet."

Anoop wrinkles his eyebrows at me. "Not like a sex partner, Romeo," he says. "For the fingerprint exercise." Blank look.

He sighs and explains. We're supposed to examine paper printouts of fingerprints. This will allow us to "become acquainted with the concept of ridges."

Alas, I move too slowly, and Raquel quickly pairs off with Hairston, of all people. She holds two of the high-powered magnifying lenses up to her face. She already has big, beautiful golden brown eyes. They are the color of a well-toasted marshmallow and just as warm and gooey. Magnified through the glass of the lenses, just the sight of them makes my heart hurt. Hairston is almost, but not quite, smiling. That dude is hard to read.

"I guess you're stuck with me, toolshed," Anoop says loudly in my direction. He is weird with cursing, like, instead of calling you "tool" he'll say "tool belt" or "toolshed." One time he called me a "multi-use hand tool." Now he's holding both magnifying glasses over his eyes, which are also big and brown. Somehow the result is not quite as fetching.

"Before we begin," Mr. Zant says, squeezing into the seat next to my rightful partner, "allow me to explain Locard's exchange principle. The great Edmond Locard was an absolute lion in the field of forensics." He continues, reading in a serious voice like a snooty professor. "The forensic scientist Paul L. Kirk best explained the exchange principle as follows: 'Wherever he steps, whatever he touches, whatever he leaves, even unconsciously, will serve as a silent witness against him. Not only his fingerprints or his footprints, but his hair, the fibers from his clothes, the glass he breaks, the tool marks he leaves, the paint he scratches, the blood or semen he deposits or collects—all of these and more bear mute witness against him.'"

I watch as Maureen turns bright red at the mention of the word "semen." She probably has a crush on dreamy, hip Mr. Zant. He is so handsome.

"Now let's collect some evidence!" Mr. Zant commands, making an upward twirling spiral in the air with the tip of his pen. As I have been trying to do for the whole hour, I catch Raquel's eye.

"The game," I blurt out, "is a-finger!"

See, because of how Sherlock Holmes said, "The game is afoot." But we were talking about *finger*prints? So I said "finger"? It doesn't get better if I explain it. Judging from the look on her face, Raquel doesn't think so either.

See why I need a manual?

Mr. Zant hands out the cards, each with an image of a fingerprint on them. All we have to do is look at them through magnifying glasses and compare them to a second set. We have to figure out which, if any, are identical. I know I'm going to be bad at it. Attention to detail is not my strong suit. Plus, I drifted off during the discussion of ridges and patterns and whorls. The patterns really are called "whorls"—that I remembered, because I thought he wrote "whores" on the board and started laughing. Especially funny was when he started talking about "double loop whores." (I mean "whorls.")

I'm playing with the magnifying glass, staring at the back of the card for some reason. I notice a dot in the lower-left-hand corner. I look closer. It's not a dot, but letters, written in a tiny font! Like maybe two-point Times New Roman. I look closely, staring with the magnifying glass. It's initials. My initials: GL.

"Hey, Anoop, look at this," I say. He is working hard, of course, examining the ever-living crap out of some whorls. "It says 'GL' on the back of my card."

"Why on earth are you looking at the *back* of the card?" he asks, peering closely and jotting notes in the fancy little leather-bound notebook he always carries.

"Just look at the back of yours," I command.

He sighs his annoying "I'm humoring you, Guy" sigh again, but he looks anyway. "Huh," he says. "It says 'TK.'" I look up and see a smile run across Mr. Zant's face. When he notices me looking, he quickly glances away and pretends to be seriously interested in a chart on the wall explaining which fish of the North Pacific are overfished.

"Uh, wuzzu?" TK says. He had heard Anoop mention his name, so looks up, perplexed.

"I wasn't saying your name, TK," Anoop says. "I was saying 'TK.'"

TK narrows his eyes.

"My name *is* TK," he says.

"I just . . . never mind," Anoop says.

"Hey, Raquel," I say, feeling bold, glad to have a reason to talk to her. "Are there initials on the back of *your* card?"

She looks up from her magnifying glass, flips her hair in a gesture so cute that I almost faint, and turns the card over.

"Yeah," she says. "It says 'MF.'"

We all laugh. Okay, mainly I laugh. Why would Zant write an abbreviation for the filthiest word possible on a card? But wait: maybe it's not that. My brain is churning away. I see a trend!

HD, MF, TK, GL . . . "Mr. Zant!" I say. "Each card has initials on the back."

"Is that right?" he asks, faking like it's news to him. He is being very kind to me. Apparently the fact that I am a dedicated practitioner of hard science (yeah, right) has compelled him to forgive me for the weird scene I caused the previous day. I resolve to be less weird. Or, you know, at least to try.

"Everyone, please look on the back of your cards with your magnifying glasses," I say. Saying "please" is classy, right? Girls like it? Maureen and TK flip their cards over while Mr. Zant grins his rakish smile.

"Mine says 'AC,'" Maureen says in her little hamster-squeak voice.

"And, uh, this says, um, 'RF,'" TK says. Hairston doesn't say anything at first, but it's pretty clear to me that he got his own card. It must say "PH" on the back. Wait, no: "HD."

"Yeah, mine says 'HD,'" mumbles Hairston. "'High Definition,' oh yeah, maybe that could be my new nickname!" Shockingly, everyone ignores him. Good try, though, Penis-Head.

"Do you see a pattern in this information?" Mr. Zant asks, smiling again. "A good deal of forensics work is recognizing patterns, whether in the whorls of a fingerprint or in the behavior of a killer."

"Those are everybody's initials!" I yell. Again, volume control is getting the best of me.

"'GL' is me, 'AC' is Anoop, 'MF' is Maureen, 'RF' is Raquel, 'HD' is Hairston, and 'TK' is, well, TK."

"That's right, Guy!" Mr. Zant says. "Now, why do you think those letters are on those cards?"

I have no idea. No one does. It is silent, the only audible noise being the click and purr of the AC overhead. (I mean the air conditioning, not Anoop Chattopadhyay. That would be weird if he were clicking and purring.)

It is Raquel who speaks up. Smart girl. "Are these, like, *our* fingerprints?" she asks. She gestures for TK to hand over the card that reads "RF" and then compares her actual digits to the print on the card, checking whorls in the flesh, I guess.

"This definitely looks like my fingerprint," she says. "Freaking weird."

Mr. Zant just smiles and then slowly walks out of the room, sneaking away like we are dozing guard dogs he doesn't want to awaken. Comments from the six of us go something like this:

"So, wait: he did all this in one day? Scanned our prints and made these cards?"

"And he didn't know who would be back today. He must have done it for everyone who was here yesterday."

"He seriously needs a life."

"Or a girlfriend."

"I nominate me."

"Shut up."

"Isn't it, like, illegal to collect our fingerprints? He needs a warrant!"

"That's only if you're arrested."

"And if he's a police officer."

"Is he?"

"Didn't you even read that form you signed? You consented to allow him to collect your fingerprints and DNA for educational purposes."

"Nah, I never read that kind of crap."

"Ew, he can collect our DNA?"

"I bet you'd like that."

"Gross!"

"So how did he get our fingerprints? What a freak!"

Then we go silent for a minute. How *did* he get our fingerprints?

Maureen, that bad MF, speaks up. "He probably lifted our fingerprints from the papers we signed yesterday," she says. "With fingerprint tape or whatever. Then he scanned them into a computer and printed them out on these cards. And it's not hard to print in a tiny font. I've done it before. Just use a word processor and set the font to like a two-point font or whatever."

"I knew it!" I yell. "Two-point Times New Roman!" I sort of like fonts. Most everyone looks at me like I am an idiot. Maureen smiles.

Then Mr. Zant sticks his head back into the classroom. "Maureen is correct," he says in a chipper voice, clapping his hands once. I guess he was listening from outside. Or he has the room bugged. "Did you enjoy today's exercise?" he asks. The whole thing was definitely on the creepy side, but all heads are nodding. We agree that we kind of did enjoy the exercise. "I think we're going to have one heck of a good year," he says. Anoop agrees. He happily files the fingerprint cards into his notebook. I'm not so sure.

"If by 'good,' you mean super-creepy to the max, Zant-O," I say, "then we're in agreement here, my friend. Yes-sir-ee . . ."

CHAPTER FOUR

Later that day I am at home, writing like mad with a pen on an old notepad. The goal is to make a record of every single thing I can remember my father ever saying to me. Or, okay, every interesting thing. I don't write down things like "Leave me alone for the next two hours, I'm planning on taking a crap the likes of which the world has never known." (Actual Francis Langman quote.) Although really, even the meaningless things feel like maybe they mean something. Isn't that what life is? A series of meaningless things? Some real gems come to mind, like the time I was upset about something and Dad responded by telling me that someday it wouldn't matter. What he actually said was, "Some day this unpleasantness will just be an ant fart in the hurricane of history." I'm writing that down. Writing and writing and writing.

I haven't worked this hard on anything in a while. I'm not one of those people who spend hours online, and I certainly am not known for spending serious blocks of time doing homework. What do I like to do most of all? Short answer: Not much. Long answer: Cartoons, video games, and bubble baths. I guess Anoop was right. If I get around to applying for college, it will be a pretty weird application. So Mom is surprised to see me working so hard.

"What's this mammoth project ya seem to be working on, GL?" she asks. I didn't even notice her come in. I don't know where she was, but she's dressed nicely—a bright blue skirt-and-jackety thing with bright gold buttons. *"War and Peace?"* she cracks.

When I tell her what I am actually working on—a collection of the wisdom of one Francis Langman—she rolls her eyes, twice. Dad has been dead less than half a year, but she has already moved past the grieving widow phase and has apparently found comfort in making fun of him as a way to bury her feelings. Hey, Dr. Waters, I don't even need to go to Slippery Rock to figure that one out.

"What time did ya start?" she asks.

"As soon as I got home," I say. "About three."

"Then I reason ya would have been done by about three oh' nuthin'." She laughs, then coughs. It echoes off the cathedral ceiling and creeps me out. I made her give up her pack-a-day habit after Dad died, but apparently the cough stays even after you quit. She's young for a mom (way younger than her deceased husband) and young-looking for her age, but she sounds old when she laughs like this. It scares me.

"Don't speak ill of the dead, Ma," I say.

"Then we pretty much can't speak of him at all, can we?" she says, her voice suddenly smooth again. She bats her eyelashes. That might sound like a harsh thing to say about your recently dead husband, but, like I said, it's her way of coping. I'm pretty sure I am going to have a weird sense of what marriage is supposed to look like. And I don't just mean that my dad was decades older than my mom, although there is that.

"Mom," I say. "Tell me Dad's life story again." I know a few things: dates and facts, names and places. I have snapshots, video clips, images of funny haircuts and tacky suits, and of course my own memories. But what about the nooks and crannies? When he was alive and would say, "Back in my day, son . . . ," I tended to tune him out.

"Where, oh where to begin?" she asks. "Your father was born in the Great Depression, and he spent the rest of his life making sure 'great depression' described his effect on the life of everyone he met." Funny. (Not really. And anyway, I know it isn't true. Dad made everyone happy, ex-girlfriends excluded. In addition to that rather lengthy list, no matter who you were—from children to ancient war veterans, from crazy hippies to billionaire businessmen—all sorts and types loved Francis Langman.) The other part is true: he was born during the Great Depression. And the year I was born minus 1929 equals the fact that my dad was clinically old by the time I was born. Right around his sixty-something birthday. Viva Viagra! Okay, that is gross.

"What else do ya wanna know?" Mom asks.

"Everything."

"GL, words can't describe that man," she says. I can tell she is trying to change the subject, but I don't feel like letting her off the hook.

"Try, Ma," I say. "What was his childhood like?"

"In Newark? He probably had a regular childhood for a Newark kid in the 1930s."

"What does that even mean?"

"How am I supposed to know? He lived many lives before he met me," she says with a dismissive hand gesture, like a bird trying to flutter away. Her gold bracelets jangle. "Probably stickball, pool halls, smoking in the boys' room. Hanging out with all the other Jews on Prince Street. Chasing girls."

■ ɜ) ■

"He was a stud," I say, laughing. Why did I say that? It sets her off.

"Oh, he was. I fell for him hard. He had a . . . a way about him . . ."

I know where the conversation is going. Since his death, she doesn't generally like to talk much about Francis, but she loves to tell tales of the romantic gestures that made up their courtship. Tales of song and dance, wine and roses, hot tubs and back rubs. Um, nope. Time to go up to my room. It seems I'm going to have to investigate the life of Francis Langman another way.

Just as I get up to my room and climb over the mountains of clothes and other junk on the floor to flick on the Atari, my phone rings. Most people just text me—only one person actually likes to chat with actual mouth-words. I don't feel much like the mouth-words, but I pick up anyway.

"Aren't you glad you signed up?" Anoop asks.

"No," I say, just because I don't want him to be all smug. I can picture him. "Are you doing the smug chin?" I ask. He laughs.

"Oh, you're glad," he says. "I can tell. You can thank me later."

"I can thank you never, Smug Chin," I say.

"You're welcome, tool-supply store," he replies. "You'll be back." I want to disagree, but I sort of know that he's right.

"Did you just call to be smug?" I ask.

"Also because I miss the sound of your voice," he says.

"Nice."

"Also, I wanted to tell your mom I'll be by later," he says. And then he stops himself. He always used to pretend he was having an affair with my mom, which was gross but funny. He's stopped since my dad died, out of respect, I guess. It's not as funny now that she's a single woman. Eesh. Just thinking about the phrase "single woman" gets me a bit teary. Screw it. I don't care if Anoop wants to talk about boning my mom. Okay, maybe I care a little.

I make small talk with Anoop for a little while longer, but I don't much feel like it. I make some excuse to get off the phone and promise him I'll see him tomorrow. I don't feel like playing video games either, really. Man, there might really be something wrong with me. I think of Dr. Waters's question: "Do you no longer enjoy things that give you pleasure?" At the time, I laughed because I thought she was talking about jerking off, but maybe there's something to it. Maybe I *am* depressed. Crap.

I feel like the walls of my room are closing in on me, so I go into the hall. It's not any better. The whole house is smothering me. I realize what it is. It's everywhere. My father. Even if Anoop hadn't made that awkward little joke, I'd be thinking about Dad. It's impossible not to think of him in that house—everything screams his name like a chorus of ghosts haunting my every step. Chairs and tables, even the carpet and the TV—all have a Francis Langman story. The crescent-moon coffee stain on the tablecloth. A drinking glass can set off a memory. Seeing one in the sink that Mom must have just had a drink out of earlier takes me back to some of the strongest memories ever.

I'll never forget the first time my father died. Or the last. Several of the ones in the middle are sort of a blur. But those two are the ones I will always remember. Francis Langman had a really dark sense of humor. There was nothing he couldn't make a joke out of. And when he started to get up there in years, "pushing eighty with both hands," as he would put it, everyone started giving him advice.

"Stop smoking."

"Watch what you eat—no fatty foods."

"Get some mild exercise—nothing strenuous."

He joked that what they were saying was, "Try not to die today."

"Why don't you just say that?" he'd ask. "Just tell me to try to avoid kicking it." Usually my mom was the one giving him advice for healthy living, so she was the one on the end of his sharp comebacks. "Why don't you just say 'Frannie—you're looking like you're about dead. Why don't you try and not die today?'"

Mom didn't really think it was all that funny. I sort of did. Although now, looking back on it, it wasn't funny at all. Did I really delude myself into thinking that his end would never come? How stupid was I? But then again, Dad was the kind of guy who honestly seemed immortal. And after all, he did die many times.

I guess I mean he "died" many times. It must have been after some fight with Mom over the contents of his nighttime ritual (two cigars and three glasses of whiskey with just a little ice) that he dreamt up the plan. I can now imagine his gruff voice as he says to himself, "If they think I'm gonna be dead, let 'em see me dead!" So one night—a rare night when I was actually out doing something (nothing exciting, just movies with Anoop)—I came back sort of late. And there was Dad, sitting on his tattered leather chair in the den with a frozen look on his withered face. His mouth was open, his eyes were fixed in a far-off gaze, and his empty glass had rolled to a stop on its side a few feet away. He was dead.

"Dad!" I screamed, my heart rocketing in my chest. I said it several times, my words punching the quiet night air. My voice started high and ended low, a descending scale of grief and sadness ending in a subsonic moan. "Dad! Dad! Dad! Dad . . ."

Mom came rushing down from her bed upstairs. She often went to bed an hour or so before the old man. She was rubbing her eyes, clutching her sleep mask, and running down the stairs, her fancy new robe trailing behind like a superhero's cape.

I tried to find the words. Tried to say, "He's dead." But the vowels stuck in my throat. I could only gasp, a sick high-pitched hiss, like when you pinch the neck of a balloon and let the air out in a whine. "Nooooooo," I finally said, the only word I could find.

And then Dad started smiling, then giggling, then full-on laughing, then shouting.

"You should see the goddamn looks on your goddamn faces! Why didn't I think to bring down a camera! Ha-ha. Goddamn priceless."

I thought Mom was going to faint. I thought *I* was going to faint. But we just stood there, our eyes leaping out of our heads like the eyes of cartoon characters. We looked at each other and then at him, back and forth, still totally stunned.

"Relax. I'm just yanking your chain," he said. "You won't believe how long I've been sitting here, Guy. I thought you said your movie ended at ten-thirty. What were you doing? Getting to second base with your boyfriend?"

"Christ," I said. And then I added, in a still-stunned whisper, "We went to the Berry Ridge Diner after."

"Well, let this be a goddamn lesson to you both," he said. "I ain't dying anytime soon. So quit worrying about me and let me live my goddamn life."

After that time, Dad "died" many more times. I can't

remember how many times I'd come home and find him playing "corpse" in some odd position or another. I'd gasp, and he'd always jump up with a laugh or an improvised song with an Irish melody: *"Hey there, Guy / You thought I'd died / But your old man lied / Your old man ain't never gonna dieeeee."* Sometimes he'd hop up and full-on break into a jig in his robe and underpants.

Except, of course, for last May, when he didn't . . .

Every room of the house is weirding me out. I decide to hide up in the attic. This is a terrible idea. It's weirding me out worse. It's filled with Dad's personal effects. Man, it's so weird how after you die, your things become your "effects." No one ever calls your things your "effects" while you're alive, do they? Maybe when you go to jail. I'm totally going to start calling my things my "effects." And I'm also totally going to start wearing an ascot. Dad has a bunch of awesome ascots among his effects. I can't quite figure out how to tie one, but it still looks cool draped across my neck. I don't look as cool as he did in all these pictures. There are a lot of pictures among his "effects." I don't think Mom has even gone through all this stuff. She jokes about him, but I don't think she likes to think too much about him being gone. I think back to the funeral. She put those sunglasses on, covered her eyes, hid her tears, and that was that. Sunglasses are totally a symbol for not dealing with shit, right, Dr. Waters?

It's hot as hell up in the attic, and dusty. There are some crazy things in here. There are the coins, of course, the literal treasure of his life. I take them out of the ancient cigar box and turn them over in my hand. They're Spanish, I think. Dad never said how much they were worth. He'd just say "a whole hell of a lot." Thousands? Tens of thousands? There are three of them.

Supposedly there were a lot more—he discovered a whole trove. He sold them soon after discovering them, and it helped make him rich. But I think he wished he'd kept them all rather than just these lucky three. There is something so awesome about them, something beyond money. They are the type of things that should probably have been kept in a safe or a bank vault or something. But Dad being Dad, they sit in a box in the attic. You can't believe the shine on three-hundred-year-old coins. I rub my thumb over the raised figures on each coin—a cross and a lion. And I can almost hear Dad telling the story about how he got them . . .

"The trip down to the Keys was almost enough to get us killed. The seas were so rough, I threw up so many times, that my stomach was empty and I began barfing up bits of bone. But I had it on good authority that a shipwreck could be found down there, and it just hadn't been found yet because the scuba technology sucked—until I improved it. I should have never sold that patent. If I was the only one with a Langman valve, I could have found countless treasures. Not that the valve didn't pay well enough. But money is nothing—it's the adventure that I loved. And this was quite an adventure. Me and my crew arrived on the island, finally. I had lost forty pounds from puking and was almost too thin for the wet suit. I was delirious and starving and it was about a thousand degrees down there. But I knew I had to get that treasure. I knew I was the only one who could complete the difficult dive. And when I did, when I laid my eyes on those chests of gold . . ."

Also up here is Dad's birth certificate and a "birth spoon," which apparently was normal to get. Hey, congratulations on being born. Have a spoon.

There is an envelope on which Dad had written BORING SHIT

in his distinctive hand. No need to look in there. Unless, hey, maybe that was his brilliant way of making sure no one would look in there. I open it up. And there are no files. Just more pictures. Mostly old pictures of Dad. There's one of him on a boat that catches my eye. Mainly because he just looks so . . . alive. So absolutely and undeniably and electrically *alive*. He's tan and shirtless, with a full head of hair and a curly beard whipping in the wind. He has his arm around a young dude I've never seen before. I'm sure I've never seen him, yet he does look oddly familiar under a scraggly beard of his own. They have their arms around each other and are laughing and smiling and . . .

"Find anything good?" Mom asks.

"You scared the hell out of me!" I yell, dropping the pictures. "I . . . I didn't hear you come up." She comes up to me and looks over my shoulder. I hold up the picture of Dad and Beard-O on the boat. "Who is this?" I ask. She reaches over and fixes the ascot around my neck. But she doesn't answer the question.

"Are you okay?" she says. The answer, I think, of course, is "Absolutely not." The answer I say, of course, is "Sure, sure, sure." It's quiet for a moment. I don't feel like small talk, but Dr. Waters says that small talk is healthy and that I should practice it even if it feels pointless and wrong and stupid. "Did I tell you I've been doing this Forensics Squad thing Anoop talked me into?" I say. "It's sort of weird, but sort of fun."

"Forensics, huh?" she says. "I always thought there were only three ensics."

"Good one," I say. My fondness for dumb jokes isn't solely a paternal trait. "Today we did fingerprints and stuff like that."

"Oh," she says. "You know I don't have any on this finger?"

She waves the index finger on her left hand at me like we're playing "Where is Thumbkin?"

"Yeah, Ma, you've mentioned it." Mom *really* likes to tell the story about how Uncle Walt talked her into touching a cigarette lighter in Grandpa's car when she was a kid. It burned the index finger on her left hand so badly and so deeply, the print never grew back.

"If I ever got fingerprinted, all they'd find would be a blur."

"Shoulda been a jewel thief, Ma," I say. That's what I always say when she tells that story.

"Shoulda," she says, which is what she always says. Silence again fills the stale attic air.

"So, who is this?" I ask, showing her the picture.

"I really don't know who that is," she says, returning her attention to the picture of Dad in my hand. She doesn't take it from me, but she stares intently. "I've never even seen this before," she says. I believe her. Big mistake.

CHAPTER FIVE

Next week's Forensics Squad begins with a buzz in the air. Every-one is still worked up about day two. How had Zant lifted our fingerprints? And why? We've lost dear Penis-Head, so we're down to five hard-core fans: me, Anoop, TK, MF, and Raquel. Oh yes, Raquel is here. The lovely Miss Flores is looking unbelievable in a thigh-high black dress and knee-high black boots. Dear Lord. I don't think I can even talk about it.

No one is saying much. Is everyone feeling overwhelmed by those boots? They are some nice boots. I might have mentioned that. Zant enters. Still quiet. It is Maureen who says something first. "Okay, so was I right?" she asks in a chirp. "You lifted our fingerprints off those papers?"

Mr. Zant nods his head yes, his auburn hair bouncing softly in the sun as he does. Shut up. "I've been at this for a while," he says. "So it wasn't that hard for me. All I had to do was dust your papers for latent prints using fingerprinting powder. Then I lifted the prints with fingerprinting tape, scanned them into my computer using a regular scanner, and printed them out on these cards. Easy-peasy."

"Easy-peasy?" I say, raising one eyebrow. Seriously?

Mr. Zant continues. "If I were really using these finger-prints for crime-solving, I would feed the prints into a special piece of software that would create a spatial map of all of your ridge patterns. The computer runs a script to put them into binary, and then can relatively quickly compare each print to the thousands that are in the databases." The nerds are impressed. Okay, I am too.

"I didn't do that, though," he continues. "Good thing, right? Catch you for all those crimes you've been a part of?" Everyone laughs.

"My mom has no fingerprints!" I blurt out. "She's not a jewel thief, though." And no one laughs. "Uncle Walt burned them off." Nice explanation. Smooth.

Then Mr. Zant continues. "Moving on," he says. Nice. "Real fingerprinting tape is expensive and real fingerprinting powder is awfully messy, but there's a way we can do a simple project to lift fingerprints. Ummm . . . Guy, would you please help me hand out these supplies?"

"Why?" I ask. "What did I do?"

"Not as punishment or anything," he says. "I just need a hand, and you're right there."

"Guy is lazy," Maureen says by way of explaining me.

"I am not!" I yell. Although yeah, I totally am. I just don't want Raquel to think of me that way. I want her to think I am an ambitious young go-getter. At least until we get married or get to second base and it is too late for her to back out.

"He's totally lazy," TK adds. (Is this something everyone knows about me? Is it because I am known in English class for my ability to write as few words as possible whenever we have to come up with sentences for vocabulary? I am seriously a master at that, especially after I realized that one-word sentences are technically sentences when used as a command. The subject is implied. For example, if you're ever asked to use the word "initiate" in a sentence just write: "Initiate." It's totally correct.)

"Fine," I say. "I'll pass out the damn supplies."

"Language, please," Mr. Zant says. "We're still in school."

"Gee, I'd love to pass out the gosh-darn supplies," I say, doing a goofy elbow-shaking dance like I'm in an old sitcom. Mr. Zant rolls his eyes.

"Anoop, maybe you can help me here, then," Mr. Zant says.

"I'll do it, I'll do it," I say, slamming my chair back harder than I meant to. It bangs into Maureen's desk.

"Sorry," I say. She rolls her eyes too. Too bad getting people to roll their eyes isn't some sort of marketable skill. I'd be a gosh-darn billionaire. So I help pass out the supplies: a few cards made of thick white paper, tape, paintbrushes, pencils, and some little handheld pencil sharpeners. The sharpeners all have smiley faces on them, which make them seem sort of morbid somehow.

Mr. Z instructs us that the first step is for each of us to use the sharpeners until we have "about a thimble's worth of graphite from the pencils." First of all: A thimble's worth? How many of us have lots of experience with thimbles? Second of all: That's an awful lot of grinding. It feels like all day, sitting there, twirling my pencil. (So to speak.)

"Sheesh," I say, shaking my hand out, faking deep pain. Really, I am just bored.

"Keep grinding, Guy," Mr. Zant says.

"Why aren't you grinding?" I ask him.

"I *wish* he was grinding," I hear a muttered voice say from the corner. I don't look out to hear from whence it came. Sometimes it's better not to know.

And we keep grinding and grinding and grinding.

And then Mr. Zant explains how to collect fingerprints. We each press our fingers into the cards, then sprinkle a thin layer of the graphite powder onto them. Anoop takes it very seriously, keeping his area very neat, like if he contaminates the operation with germs a patient might die or something. I keep faking like I am going to sneeze on Anoop's card. I'm hilarious.

"And now please be very delicate as you brush away enough powder so that a print becomes visible. Voilà!" he says.

"Voilà?" I ask.

"Voilà."

"You don't get to say that word too much," I say.

"Maybe you don't—I say it all the time. Maybe there's just something wrong with the way you're living your life, Guy, if you don't have a lot of 'voilà' moments. You should have at least one 'voilà' moment a day—probably ten or more at your age."

I want to give him the finger and shout "Voilà, dickhead!" but instead I just mumble "Whatever" and get on with the project.

I have to admit, it is sort of cool to see my whorls developing right there on the card. I am not as good at it as Anoop, of course. He seems born to perform this type of delicate operation. I just do okay. I Langman my way through it enough that I get the basic idea.

"If you don't properly lift the print," Mr. Zant says, "if you don't pay attention to every detail, if protocols aren't followed—if a sample is misplaced, if the chain of custody is broken—it's no small thing. A killer could go free."

"Weeee-oooh," I say. Everyone gives me a look. "Scary ghost noise," I explain. No one seems to find this explanation sufficient. "Voilà!" I add. That does it. Yup.

CHAPTER SIX

After Anoop drops me off at home, I feel sort of like complete and total shit. Forensics Squad is cool, but it's weirding me out, the talk of death. Like dying is just a game, a puzzle to be solved. It's really not. I wish Dad were here. As if I need a reminder that it's not a game. What is the point of it all? He's the only one I want to ask. So you know what? I decide to go visit him. Mom's not home, and I don't drive. Even though it's raining, my only choice is to walk. I don't mind. It isn't raining hard, just tiny drops fluttering like fleas. You hardly notice them until suddenly you are soaked and you have no idea why. I am starting to notice details, I realize. Mr. Zant is getting into my head.

The closer I look at the rain, the more I can see the tiny individual drops swooping down and swirling around in several directions at once, like even the weather is feeling confused. I sure feel that way. I feel totally alone. Like a piece of paper soaked in water and run over by a car. It's a long walk to Berry Ridge Cemetery. *We all end up at Berry Ridge Cemetery.*

The cemetery where Dad is buried is in a tacky place—just off the shoulder of one of the busiest roads in Berry Ridge's commercial district. This being America, we have to have at least one street with fourteen fast-food joints on it. This being Berry Ridge, they are sort of fancy-looking fast-food joints with pillars out front and expensively manicured flower beds and stuff. But it is still the tackiest part of town. And there, just off the shoulder of the busy road, sits a large cemetery. A lot of people are annoyed that more and more fast-food places and tacky billboards are going up alongside the final resting place of their loved ones, but I know that somehow Dad wouldn't have cared.

What's everybody all balled up about? I could imagine him asking. *That their dead relatives would give a rat's ass about traffic noise? I think they've probably got bigger problems. Like being dead, for instance.* Ha-ha. That's a totally made-up Francis Langman quote, but definitely the type of thing he would have said. It would have been fun to say it to him. To have the wise/smart-assy words come out of my mouth and go to his ears. To see if they would have made him laugh. So I go ahead and say them. Out loud.

I never thought I'd be one of those people who talks to a dead person at a cemetery, but there, in the parklike setting under the magnolia trees, flanked by the traffic noise, raindrops dripping off my nose—there I find myself talking to my father. The place where he's buried is marked only by a stone. Not even his name. He requested it that way, which was odd. There is no wacky inscription like he used to joke about. He used to say he wanted his tombstone to read FRANCIS LANGMAN: MAN, THAT DUDE COULD DANCE! or FRANCIS LANGMAN: THE JEWISH COCKHORSE. (I don't even know—nor do I want to know—what that means.) Nothing at all marks his eternal resting place, but it's easy to find his plot. I feel like I know his neighbors—Edith Wasikowski and Peter Jay Harvington. Plus, Fran is right under the Burger King sign crassly shouting about chicken clubs and burgers.

I find myself standing there in the dribbles of rain. "Hi, Dad," I say. Then I tell him my joke about the dead people giving a rat's ass about the traffic noise. And I tell him that he'd probably think I was "nuttier than a squirrel turd" for talking to him, but I feel like doing it anyway.

And I start to tell him everything. About school and Mr. Zant. About Raquel and Forensics Squad. About the strange people at his funeral. About the mysterious pictures in the attic. And about what I think deep down sometimes. What I never tell anyone. About how sometimes I am not really sure if life is worth living. And I know what they say: Talking to yourself is one thing, but when you start answering back is when you really should start to worry. But I do it anyway. I start saying his parts back to myself. I know. Nuttier than a squirrel turd.

"What's the point of all this, Dad?" I ask him. I gesture around the cemetery, pointing at the trees, the sky, the grass, the bench a few feet away.

"I think the point of that bench is that it's a place to put your ass when you get tired," he says.

"You know what I mean," I say. "Of all of it. Life."

"Life ain't a pencil, Guy. It ain't gotta have a point."

"But then what are we living for?" I ask.

"You got someplace else you need to be? What the hell else are we going to do?" he asks. "Stick our dicks in bowling balls?"

"You got a point there," I say.

"Listen, son," he continues. "Life ain't easy, but it don't got to be hard neither. Do these things: First of all, take care of your mother. She needs you. Secondly, be good to your friends. They are one of the few things in life that are truly worth something. And follow your heart. It knows what's right. Certainly more than your balls."

CHAPTER SEVEN

I'm waiting for Mr. Zant to hurry up and finish. Ironically, his lesson is something about how we need patience to be good at forensics. But I don't want to listen to the lesson; I want to get to work on my own project this week. And I need Mr. Zant's help.

"Every single drop of blood, every hair, every tiny bit of evidence, must be numbered and labeled," he says. "You will need to reference these later. A simple mix-up in your paperwork could set a killer free. Every piece of evidence must follow a closely watched chain of custody. If someone who is not supposed to have access ends up so much as touching or in some cases even breathing on the evidence, it will likely be thrown out of court. And okay, that just about wraps it up. We are out of time."

Everyone starts to gather their things and make their way out into the hallway. "You probably loved that talk about needing patience, Guy, huh?" Anoop says.

"Shut up," I say.

"You're the least patient person I know."

"Well, now I need *you* to be patient. Just wait up. I need to talk to Mr. Zant."

"What about?" Mr. Zant says, overhearing me.

"Yeah, what about?" Anoop says.

"Dude," I say to Anoop. "Some things are private."

"Ooh, private!" Mr. Zant says, clapping his hands.

"Yeah, Anoop. Wait in the hall." Anoop gives me a very quizzical look, sighs and huffs, but like a good friend goes to wait in the hall.

Mr. Zant turns to me and freaks me out. "Solving a crime isn't all paperwork," he says. "Sometimes it's hunches. I can tell already—you have the right hunches. You could be good at crime-solving if you learn to do the work."

Compliments make me feel awkward, so I let the latter part of his comment slide, even though it does feel sort of good. I have good hunches? Thanks, Zant. I have a hunch you're weirding me out.

"Yeah, um, thanks," I say. "So listen. I wonder if you could help me process some evidence." Now it's his turn to give me a quizzical look. I carry on. "If I have some old pictures and I want to figure out who is in them, what's the best thing to do?"

"Do you have an exemplar?" he says, stroking his beard.

"Do you like saying words I don't know?"

"We talked about exemplars last week."

"I wasn't paying attention . . . that . . . week?"

"Exemplars are something to compare them to."

"No, I don't have anything to compare them to. They're just some old pictures. My dad was with some guy and I want to know who he was. Is. If he still is."

"Alive?"

"Yeah."

"Well, there's not much we can really do, but if you want to bring them in, it might be an interesting exercise."

"I hate exercise," I say.

"I knew you'd say that," he says.

"But I do have the pictures with me," I say. I take out the old picture of my father and the mysterious other man on the boat. "I have a feeling I know this guy," I say, pointing to the non-Dad guy. "But I can't figure out why. If you had a picture of someone and you wanted to know who they are, what do you do?"

Mr. Zant looks at the photograph a long time. He handles it gently, careful to only touch the edges. "It's very hard," he says. "Maybe if this were a police investigation, they'd run the picture through some facial recognition software. But that only works if you have something to compare it to."

"Isn't there some software you can run that would show what the person would look like thirty years later?" I ask.

"Sure there is," Mr. Zant says. "But I don't think we need to."

"What do you mean?" I say.

"Guy," he says. "In thirty years the person on the left will look like the person on the right."

"What?" I ask again, even though I think I already know where he's going with this.

"Look at the eyes. Look at the nose. Look at the shape of the eyes and the lips. They're almost identical. The younger man is clearly the older man's son." I feel my face turn red. I feel my temperature drop fifty degrees. I start to shake.

"Guy!" Mr. Zant says. "Are you all right?" I'm not, of course, but I try to compose myself. I take a deep breath and steady myself on the desk. Dad had another son? Why didn't I see it? And why didn't Mom see it? She saw this picture the other day, when I was holding it. Was it really the first time she saw it? Did she really never see the picture before? Deep breaths, deep breaths.

"Thank you, Mr. Zant," I say. "I'm fine. Can you help me with one more thing?"

"Sure, Guy."

"Can we fingerprint this picture?"

"Well," he says. "I suppose we could. But remember, finger-printing isn't a magic bullet. It won't tell you much. It won't tell you anything at all if you don't have something to compare it to."

"I know that," I say. "And I do have something to compare it to. There are my prints, of course. But I bet you'll find a few more. The only one I care about is the one with the smudge in the middle."

"A smudge?"

"Yeah," I say. "Almost like the picture was handled by some-one who has no fingerprints at all."

Mr. Zant gives me a serious look, narrowing his eyes and purs-ing his lips. Then he smiles and skips off toward the cabinet in the corner of the room. He swings open the metal door and pulls out a small box. It's his fingerprinting kit. He opens it carefully and extracts a few items. He offers me a pair of rubber gloves. "I'm good," I say.

"Come on," he says. "You can help. It will be fun."

I'm skeptical, but I shrug and do it. The gloves feel weird, all tight and sweaty. I keep wiggling my fingers.

"You get used to it," Mr. Zant says.

"Spend a lot of time wearing rubber gloves, do you?" I ask. "Sounds like you have an interesting home life." He laughs, but doesn't answer my question.

"Okay, now we need to lightly dust the picture," he says. He shakes, then opens, a tiny blue bottle marked FINGERPRINTING

POWDER. The lid has a small brush attached to it, sort of like a bottle of rubber cement. He hands it to me.

"No, no, you do it," I say. "I don't want to mess it up."

"Messing things up is the only way anyone ever learns anything," he says. "Why do you think surgeons practice on cadavers?" I can't really argue with that logic. It seems like it might fit in the book, even if Dad didn't say it. I take the brush from his hand. I drop it on the desk, leaving a large blot of a black mark on the desk.

"Sorry!" I say.

Mr. Zant shrugs. "These desks were built to withstand nuclear war, so I think a little bit of dust is okay." I start to dab the brush toward the top right corner of the back of the picture. "Tell me why you chose that spot to start with," he says.

"I'm sorry, is that wrong?" I ask.

"Not at all," he says. "That's how most people would handle a picture, so that's the spot where you're most likely to find a print. It's the perfect place to dust for prints."

"That's what I was thinking," I say.

"Good work," he says. "Now, not too much dust. You really just need the tiniest amount. The next step is to carefully lift the print with the tape."

I take the fingerprinting tape and carefully set it onto the picture. I feel like a surgeon. It's pretty fun. But when I lift the tape up, all I see is a blurry mess.

"Ah," I say. "I told you I'd screw it up."

"No, you were perfect," he says. "That's just what we call overlap. It just means there are a bunch of prints on top of one another."

"Hey," I say. "If the person we're looking for is left-handed, they'd probably handle the opposite corner, right?"

"Right!" he says. "Is he left-handed?"

"*She*," I say. "*She* is left-handed."

I repeat the process, this time lifting a print from the top left-hand corner of the back of the picture. Like magic, a print appears before my eyes. The ridges and whorls—they are all visible. So too is the blank space in the middle.

"I can't believe it," Mr. Zant says. "It *is* almost like this person doesn't have a fingerprint on that finger . . . I've never seen anything like it, but it's just like you predicted. You *do* have the hunches, Guy! Now tell me what it means."

Before I can explain to Mr. Zant that I know exactly who the mysterious left-handed, no fingerprint woman is, Anoop sticks his head back in the door. "I really have to go, you guys," he says. "Train Chattopadhyay is leaving the station, Guy. Get aboard or you're on your own."

"Thanks a million, Mr. Zant," I say, tucking the picture back into the envelope. "I guess I gotta run. I'll give you the scoop tomorrow."

"Now would you tell me what *that* was all about?" Anoop asks as we walk toward his car. But I don't want to. There's only one person I want to talk to about this. Luckily, I know right where she lives.

CHAPTER EIGHT

"Where are the other six, GL?" Mom says after hearing me slam the door and taking one look at my flaring nostrils. I know what she means. I don't hide anger well. I'm not even past the foyer yet, just standing there inside the big front door, looking up at her. She's smiling, trying to be funny. She knows I am feeling grumpy, thus the question. It's something Dad would say when someone was in a bad mood. His joke was that you were Grumpy of the Seven Dwarfs, so the other six must be around somewhere. I would usually quickly make up where I thought all the others were. I knew he meant it rhetorically, but I couldn't resist the exercise no matter how bad a mood I was in. I would start counting on my fingers and say something like, "Sleepy is in bed, of course; Sneezy is at the allergist; Doc is on the golf course; Bashful is hiding under the rug again; Dopey—well, even he doesn't know where he is; and . . . crap." I'd always forget at least one. And yes, I realize that the fact that I usually forgot Happy probably meant something.

But no matter what, just doing that little thing would usually make me laugh. Especially if I came up with something really strange—like "Bashful is breaking out of his routine by auditioning to be a stripper"—that cracked Dad up. Just seeing him laugh would immediately snap me out of it and I couldn't remember why I was Grumpy in the first place. He'd try to play it straight, his serious deep-set eyes burning before a twinkle and the greatest laugh you've ever heard. Damn, I miss him.

But my grumpiness isn't going away so easily this time. "Grumpy" doesn't even begin to describe it. I'm pissed. There's no other way to put it. So I just blurt it out. The words come out like an auctioneer rattling off prices for a used clock or like a single word, the world's longest hyphenated one. "Mom-I-know-Dad-had-another-son-and-I-know-you-knew-and-I-can't-believe-you-never-told-me-and-I-saw-the-picture-and-I-know-you-saw-that-picture-before-the-other-day-so-don't-lie-just-tell-me-how-you-knew-and-also-tell-me-why-you-never-told-me."

She stands there, staring at me for a minute, blinking. She purses her lipsticked lips, then exhales slowly. She doesn't say anything, though. So I take the picture out from my backpack. "This younger guy is clearly Dad's son," I say. "And I fingerprinted the picture—I know you've touched it."

"You did what?" she says, almost laughing.

"It's not funny!" I say. I feel like a toddler.

"Okay, you're right." She smooths her hair, smooths the creases in her dress. If she thinks she can smooth everything away, she's wrong. I scowl. "Settle down," she says. "Have a seat."

"I don't want to have a seat!" I say. I realize I'm yelling.

"Guy," she says. "Oh, honey. I understand."

Bullshit. "How can you understand? How can anyone understand unless they learn that their whole life is a lie? What else don't I know?"

"That's it," she says. "I promise. And really, it's not like what you think."

"What I think is that Dad had a kid and never told me about it. I have a brother I never knew!"

"Well then, I guess it is what you think," she says. *Is she trying to be funny?* "I wanted to tell you a long time ago," she says. "But your father . . . he made me promise. It was a serious sore point for him. You know he loves you—he hated that he had a child he lost touch with. But his mother didn't want anything to do with your father. Your father tried to have a relationship with him, but it just didn't happen. And the boy—well, the man—he has had some . . . problems over the years. I don't think anyone in the family had seen him for decades before the funeral."

"What? He was at the funeral?"

"Yes, that strange man in the beard."

"Why didn't anyone tell me?"

"Your father never wanted you to know. And honestly, I don't want anything to do with him. He's not well."

"What do you mean, 'not well'? What do you mean, he has problems?"

"Drug problems," she says. "That's part of the reason why your father never wanted you to know about him, really. I mean, that sounds awful, but really it's just that he didn't want you to try to get close to him. He's crazy, his mother is crazy—they're all crazy, to be honest. I was surprised he's not in a room with padded walls, to tell you the truth . . . Now, I know it's a lot to take in, but please try not to worry about it. And please don't contact him."

"Try not to worry about it? Who were those other guys at the funeral? More secret relatives?"

"I honestly don't know," she says. "Your father lived a lot of lives before me. And I don't think it's a good idea for you to go back to that Forensics Squad. I don't like you digging up ancient history, obsessing on death. It's not healthy."

I say nothing. What I think is this: *Dumb move, Mom. If you wanted to make sure that I did stay in Forensics, that's all you'd have to say.*

I spend the rest of the evening doing my best to ignore Mom and the world. I go up to my room and just pace and think and then eventually fall asleep. So then, of course, when it's time to actually go to bed for the night, I'm wide-awake. All these weird thoughts are running through my mind. How can I really write a book of my dad's advice if I don't know anything about his life? What good would it accomplish? Am I trying to bring him back from the dead with this project? Just saying that word—"dead"— or thinking it, rather, is still hard for me. As that dreaded word enters my mind, I feel my eyes go dark, like I can't process the word while thinking of it. How could I have avoided it for the past sixteen and three-quarters years? Just as life is all around, so too is death.

"Okay," I tell myself. "Quit being so glum, GL. You're gonna end up wearing bondage pants and looking like a raccoon if you keep up on this morbid path." Working on this book will allow me to spend time in the company of the man, or pretend to, any-way. And once it is completed, I could leaf through the pages, drown myself in his words, and live the lie that he is still alive.

But what do I know about the man? What do I *really* know? I know his father's name was Guy. That I definitely know. It is a conversation we had many times whenever I would complain. Why would I complain? Because it's the twenty-first century and my name is Guy! "It's a good name, Guy," Dad would say. "A war-rior name. The name of my father. The name of Guy Fawkes. The name of Guy de Maupassant. The name of Sir Guy of Gisborne." (I have no idea who these people are.)

I also know his mom's name was Lana. "Lana Langman." Every time her name came up, Dad would do the "say it ten times fast" challenge. Lana Langman. Lana Langman. Lana Langman. Lana Langman. Lana Langman. Lana Langman. Lana Langman. Lana Langman. Lana Langman. Lana Langman. Sounds like total gibberish. Still cracks me up. Good stuff. But I don't know enough!

I get up and grab a notebook. I flip to a blank page and stare at it, its white rectangular form looking to me like a tombstone of pure marble. It is up to me to write an epitaph. Maybe this book isn't just going to be a list of funny/wise things Dad said. Maybe it's going to be more. Maybe it's going to tell all of it. All of him. Maybe all of me. I begin to write. My sweaty fingers struggle to grip the pen as I write those all-powerful words: CHAPTER ONE.

"Rules for Living": The Francis Langman Story
CHAPTER ONE

"It is what it is." —FRANCIS LANGMAN

Francis Langman of Berry Ridge, New Jersey, was born in Newark in 1929. His parents were Guy and Lana Langman. Say "Lana Langman" ten times fast. Guy's nickname was "Wolf," but no one knows why. They lived in Newark and worked in a clothing shop.

Francis, aka "Fran the Man" [okay, no one called him that but himself], entered this world at the beginning of the Great Depression but lived a happy young life of stickball and chasing girls. He hung out with the other Jews on Prince Street and once got kicked out of synagogue for yelling "Jesus Christ, could someone turn on a fan?" Well, it was hot in there.

From these modest beginnings he would build a life of unusual richness, traveling the globe and banging a lot of hot ladies. He knocked up some lady and had a son! Jerk. He became a scuba diver, invented the Langman valve using his knowledge of bagel making, and supposedly had a brief career as a bullfighter. Although here possibly the author is thinking of Ernest Hemingway. Pretty sure he smoked weed back then. That is, Francis. Possibly Hemingway too. Probably. How else would he justify that beard?

On one scuba trip, Francis discovered sunken treasure. Who does that? Francis Langman, that's who. He sold most of the very valuable Spanish coins, but saved three in an old cigar box. He invested most of the earnings. Some schemes made him money and some lost him money. ("Never do business in a country where the national currency is goat," he once said. Useful advice.) One smart move: he started buying property with some extra cash in North Jersey and NYC in the 1970s and it would make him a rich man.

Later, he became a father a second time. This son, Guy, would also like to travel the globe and bang lots of hot ladies, or at least bang a lot of hot ladies. For the most part, he spends his time *playing video games and arguing with nerds about murder.*

It's clear that there are some holes in this book. And there is only one way to fill in the gaps. First I have to find my long-lost brother the possible psychopath. I have some serious research to do.

CHAPTER NINE

I ponder that mystery for a while, then another mystery presents itself. It begins like this: At the next session of Forensics Squad, Mr. Z writes on the board THE FORENSIC ART OF HANDWRITING. Woo-hoo. Who among us doesn't love handwriting? I mean handwriting?! It's like writing! With your hands! I'll stop now. The Big Z begins with a few prepared remarks. "You can try, but you can't really change your handwriting," he says. "Once you learn how to form letters, it's hardwired into your brain in a complicated process. Even people who lose both arms and end up writing with their mouths eventually develop a handwriting—or should I say mouth-writing—style that is very similar to the way they wrote when they had their hands . . ."

This *is* sort of interesting, and I look around the room to see everyone's reactions. TK casts his eyes about suspiciously and then puts his pen in his mouth and starts writing something. He shrugs and seems pleased with the results of his experiment. Maureen has a very serious look on her face. Raquel is not paying much attention at all. As usual, she is flipping through her purse, as if it's a magical container that somehow holds all the crap in the world in its minute interior. Maybe it does.

Something Mr. Zant says catches Raquel's attention. She suddenly is very interested. In fact, she raises her hand. Mr. Zant seems a bit stunned to see her offering to participate. "Yes!" he says with too much enthusiasm, pointing at her with the double-gun hand gesture.

What she has to say is: "I don't know if you know this about me, but I can totally write with my feet."

Mr. Zant laughs. It is pretty funny to consider, and rather unexpected. He doesn't know what to say. "My notes don't mention foot-writing" is all he can come up with, turning his cards over in his hands as if some answers of his own might be hidden there somewhere. "But I assume it's somewhat similar to handwriting. Or maybe you could fool forensics experts by writing a ransom note with your foot!" She giggles. "But let it be clear that I am not advocating kidnapping, class," he adds with a honking laugh.

"I might kidnap *someone*," she says, under her breath. And I sort of feel like she's looking in my direction. But maybe not actually talking to me. Or about me. What is going on here? Who does she like? I can't think about it for much longer, because I suddenly get very distracted. "Want me to show you?" she asks. "I can write on the board with my hand and then my foot and you can judge the difference," she offers.

"Wow, you can even write on the chalkboard with your toes?" Mr. Zant says. "This I have to see."

He throws the cards onto his desk, letting them cascade in a messy splay. We have clearly moved beyond little-card territory and know it. He pulls his teacher's chair around to the middle of the board and brushes it off. Then he positions the chair so that a person's feet could reach the bottom of the board. Raquel gets up, sits in his chair, then slowly removes her shoe. Her foot is tan and flawless like the rest of her. Her nails, however, are painted a shocking shade of neon blue.

I suddenly pray that I'm not called up to the board for any reason.

Raquel kicks her foot into the air like a dancer. I can't stop staring at that foot. It makes me blush. Is it weird to be turned on by a foot? What the hell?

"Oh," Mr. Zant says. He seems a little distracted by this foot as well, but tries to regain the clinical tone of a scientist while half stuttering and saying "uh" literally every other word. "First, uh, we, uh, need, uh, to, uh, get, uh, a, uh, sample, uh, of, uh, your, uh, regular, uh, handwriting, uh, as, uh, the, uh, control group, uh."

"Right," she says, picking up the chalk in her right hand. "What should I write?"

"Just, uh, whatever, uh, comes, uh, to, uh, mind, uh," he says, still unable to get the "uh" under control while Raquel's bare foot dangles in his chair.

"Write 'Raquel is a flirt,'" Maureen mutters from the corner. She doesn't mean it, of course, but Raquel writes just that in big, loopy handwriting.

Raquel is a flirt.

"Okay," Mr. Zant says, somehow able to actually complete two syllables without uh-ing. "Now write the same words with your foot for the comparison sample."

Raquel holds her foot up in the air, supporting her thigh with her hands, fireman-carry style. Mr. Zant full-on blushes as he positions a long piece of yellow chalk between her first and second toes. She leans back, tosses her hair, and slowly begins to draw letters on the board. Truth is, the handwriting (foot-writing?) is actually oddly similar to the script she had written by hand. *Raquel is a flirt, Raquel is a flirt* it says in near-identical writing. Something about it seems wrong to me, however. I remember the note she had given Anoop back at the beginning of Forensics Squad.

"Don't forget to dot the 'i' with a heart!" I say, loudly because I am nervous. Raquel gives me a confused look.

"Oh my God, gross," she says. "I never do that. Not since like fifth grade, anyway." I look over at Anoop, who is suddenly staring intently at his notebook, making intricate scribbles with his pen.

"Mr. Zant," I say, raising my hand and addressing him although I am stressing certain words that I want to make sure Anoop hears. "Doesn't that shoot a hole in your theory—that handwriting never changes? She *used* to write a heart over the letter 'i' instead of a dot, and now, suddenly, she's stopped doing that. Never does it, in fact. Isn't that *interesting?*"

Anoop gets up and runs out, muttering, "Bathroom."

"Yes, uh, that is interesting, Guy," Mr. Zant says. "I suppose that is one of those exceptions contained within every rule. Perhaps some more forensics research needs to be conducted on the evolution of handwriting in preteen girls with regards to the 'i' heart. Feel free to take that up as a research project. I'll help you get it into a good journal!"

From behind me I can hear Maureen snickering. "What?" I say.

"The day you'll see Guy do the hard work required to publish a scientific paper is the day you'll see me . . . um . . ."

She apparently can't think of the right unlikely event in her own life to compare with me writing a scientific paper. Unfortunately for her, everyone else *easily* can think of several things.

"Wearing a dress?"

"Not being a weirdo?"

"Kissing a boy? I mean an actual living boy?"

"Writing a three-page paper rather than five when the assignment is to write a three-to-five-page paper?"

"Going out into the sun without melting?"

"Ceasing to be a medium-sized, omnivorous mammal native to North America?"

This last zinger, delivered in loud volume, is mine. It's probably rude and not even all that funny, but ever since Maureen came to school with two dark circles of makeup around her eyes (apparently in an attempt to look Goth, although probably not doing it quite right), I like to find every reason to accuse her of being a raccoon. That kind of thing cracks me up. I even memorized the definition of "raccoon." See, I'm not lazy when inspired.

"Shut up!" Maureen yells. "The point here is that Guy is never going to publish a freaking scientific paper, and the process by which preteen girls stop writing hearts over the letter 'i' has to be the dumbest idea for a paper I ever heard, anyway." She slams her fist down onto her desk with more force than seems necessary. Her oddly angled ponytail pops some stray hairs from its holder. Then she collects herself, fixes the hair, and adds, "No offense, Mr. Zant."

"None taken," he says. "And for what it's worth, I don't think you're an omnivorous mammal native to North America."

"Um, thanks?"

"You're welcome, Miss Fields."

And with that strange conclusion, Forensics Squad is over for the day. Anoop, and thus my ride, is nowhere to be found. I wait impatiently for a few minutes. He went to the bathroom like twenty minutes ago. What did he do, fall in? Zing! I have things to ask him. While waiting, I try to make small talk with the nerds, who have still not left either. It seems they're talking about blood. Um, yeah.

"What are you dudes talking about?" I ask Maureen and TK.

She says nothing, just folds her arms.

"Come on," I say.

"Blood," she says, as if that's a normal answer.

"Should have guessed," I say.

"It's exciting!" she says.

"I guess," TK says, stifling a yawn.

"Blood has magic. I really believe that," she says. "Black magic."

"Like I said, it's just water and dissolved proteins," he says. "Not that there's anything wrong with water and dissolved proteins—we need them to live—but magic? Hardly."

"I really think if you had someone's blood, you could control them," Maureen says. I haven't ever seen her so animated. Her eyes are darting around like little wild animals.

"Control them?" he scoffs. "Like a voodoo doll? You are a better scientist than that."

I laugh. Can you believe it? They actually discuss things like being "a better scientist" than something. Unbelievable. And seriously, why *would* Maureen want to control someone? While she talks with TK, I notice that she is scribbling in her black notebook. It seems that she is always scribbling in a black notebook. The pages are even black, and she uses some sort of secret ink that I guess you have to read under a black light or something.

Of course I don't really care what she is writing, but you know, a black notebook filled with notes in black ink is sort of intriguing. Black ink on black pages: my life, maybe.

Anoop sticks his head into the room and says, "Dude, there you are," as if I were the one missing. "Let's get out of here," he adds. You can't hide in the bathroom forever.

"Sure," I say. He starts talking about how he got into a game he was playing on his phone, something to do with throwing knives.

We get into the AC Machine. Anoop's car, known to one and all (or okay, just to me) as "the AC Machine," is a pretty dorky mid-level sedan that would not look out of place in the teachers' lot. Where is the law written that all teachers have to drive the exact same silver sedan? For a touch of class, however, Anoop always has three or four throw pillows in the back of his car. Like fluffy red pillows with beaded trim. He claims it gives the sedan a "homier" appearance. Seriously.

I can't talk too much smack about Anoop's car, though, since I am one of the few non-freshmen at Very Rich who doesn't have any sort of car at all. Cars mean a lot here. Raquel has an awesome car—a bright red Lexus hybrid. Hip, stylish, environmentally friendly. What more could a guy ask for?

I know it is a serious hit to my status that I am car-free, but I don't really care about my status (anymore), and besides, I find that I'm going the same place as Anoop ninety-nine percent of my life anyway. Plus, yeah, I might kind of be too lazy to study for the Driver's Ed exam. There's, like, a booklet, and you have to wait in line at the DMV, and the class is, like, Saturday mornings, and . . .

So I cruise home in the AC Machine, waiting for the right moment to confront Anoop about the day's revelations. Forensics genius that I am, a few things have become abundantly clear, resulting in a feeling I don't know what to do with. It is an unusual feeling, being pissed at Anoop. Sure, sometimes he takes two turns in a row in Yars' Revenge, and sometimes he farts in my general direction with the force of an Indian elephant, but I've never really been mad at him. Not ever. And when I think about the ruse he obviously pulled, there is simply no way I can't be angry with him.

I don't like confrontation either, but it has to be said. So before we are even out of the parking lot, I just snap and let it out.

"Dude, tell me the truth. Raquel didn't really write that note, right?"

"Um, um, what?" he says. I'm right. I know it right away. Anoop is one of those people who never say "um." He's a total smooth talker who always has the right word at the ready. So it is obvious he is just buying time. I pounce! Not literally! But I don't let him stall.

"She said that she hasn't dotted an 'i' with a heart since *fifth grade*," I say. "Your ruse is out!"

"Maybe she was, um, you know, ummm . . ."

"Dude."

"Fine," Anoop says. "Fine. It *was* me who wrote that letter. But I didn't do it just as a ruse—nice word, by the way, total SAT prep word—I did it for you."

"Now this I gotta hear," I say. "Why one dude would forge a love letter to another dude who was supposedly his friend, knowing full well that that dude—"

"Just because—"

"Let me finish!" I yell. "Knowing full well that that dude could be manipulated by the girl the other dude was . . . Wait, what am I saying? I mean, why you would forge a note from a girl you knew I liked, knowing full well that it would make me so crazy in love with her that her foot could give me a boner?"

"I didn't know it would make you *crazy*," he says. "That foot-boner is on you. Some people can like girls without totally going nuts over it. I just knew that it would make you come to Forensics Squad. I knew that if I left it up to you, you'd be too lazy to ever come and spend your time doing anything other than ancient video games and bubble baths. The truth is, my friend, yeah, I wanted you there so I'd have someone to hang out with, but it's not just that."

"What?"

"I've been—I've been worried about you," he says. "This was the first thing you seemed to care about in forever, and then, after one bad day, you wanted to quit? I wanted the old you back. You haven't been the old you since . . ."

I know what he means. And what can I say? Maybe the old me died the day they put my father into that box.

"Foot-boner," I say contritely. "Good one."

He smiles. My mind sits teetering on a knife-edge. I'm pissed at Anoop for treating me like some sort of project, but I'm happy about the fact that I have someone in my life who cares so much. It falls toward happiness, but I don't feel like letting it get too sappy in the AC Machine. I decide to just make a joke out of all of it. I know, I know, Dr. Waters.

"I don't need the extracurricular thing," I say. "I don't plan to go to college," I say. "I have what's known in the business as a 'sugar daddy,'" I say.

"You mean you're, like, a 'kept boy'?'" he says.

"Sure, something like that," I say.

"Who's your daddy?" he asks in a hilariously deep voice.

"Aww, yeah," I say. I waggle my eyebrows at him. He laughs.

"Seriously, though," he says. Those have to be Anoop's two favorite words in the whole English language. Seriously, though. Seriously, though. Seriously, though. "I'm going to be rich, yeah, but I'm not going to support your ass our whole lives in some sort of hetero life-partner-type scenario forever."

"Who said anything about it being hetero?" I say in a weird voice. I don't want to let it get serious. Enough "seriously, though." Seriously. Then I purr like a cat. "Meow, Bengal Tiger," I say, lifting my eyebrows extra high. Anoop usually thinks this sort of shtick is hilarious. He'd usually be LOL-ing, for sure.

"I guess I'll come back," I say. "If Raquel is going to be my wife, I need to get on that."

Anoop exhales slowly. Now the knife teeters the other way. I'm pissed again. Beyond pissed. Because I have a hunch I know what's coming. "Don't say it," I say.

He says it.

"Guy, Raquel and I have been hanging out."

"Hanging out?"

"You know, talking and stuff."

"On dates?"

"Well, yeah, one or two. I mean, nothing serious, but it's sort of going in that way. We agreed not to tell you because we thought you would get upset . . ."

"Why would I get upset?" I yell. "Just because my supposed best friend totally stabbed me in the back like some sort of, um, back-stabby backstabber?"

"Calm down, Guy."

"Calm down? Screw that. What the hell, Anoop? You know I love her!"

"You don't love her, Guy. You never even talked to her."

"You're the one who encouraged me to go for her in the first place!"

"I just wanted you to come to Forensics. I didn't know how things would happen. I didn't know I'd end up falling for her. And I certainly didn't know that she would end up falling for me!"

The words slosh around in my brain, slow-motion-like. "Raquel." "Fell." "For." Anoop. WTF-ing F?

If Anoop weren't driving, I think I would punch him in the face. Instead, I punch the dashboard. Hard. It leaves a dent and it hurts my hand. I scream.

"Dude," Anoop says quietly. And that's all he says for the rest of the ride. Eventually we arrive at Langman Manor. And no, my house isn't really some sort of estate. It's just a big house. But yes, Dad did buy a weird sign that says LANGMAN MANOR, which he hung in the yard and we never bothered to take down. It is sort of funny, sort of a thumbing of our noses at the snooty neighbors. The sign is a bit faded, maybe more than a bit faded. The white paint has flecked off to the point where it more or less says LAG NOR against a dark green board. My mom always hated it, but it's not going anywhere. This I know.

"You suck, Anoop," I say as I get out of the car. I slam the door and storm off, feeling like it was a pretty cool exit. But then

I realize that I have forgotten my backpack. Stupid backpack. I am definitely looking forward to a stage in life that does not require a backpack. If you ever see anyone carrying a backpack, you know that their life sort of sucks. No matter how old they are. Probably definitely if they're over thirty. I reach back in and grab it. Backpack-related exits are rarely cool. So I add, "You double-suck," which is certainly a dumb thing to say. So I say it twice.

CHAPTER TEN

Next week's session of Forensics Squad. I'm here and Anoop is not. Did he quit FS? I've been avoiding him a lot lately. Who cares if he did. But what am I even doing here? And how am I going to get home? Why didn't I think of that before I had a fight with him? Or at least before I decided to stay late without a ride home. I try texting Mom again, but she's not responding. What is she up to? And Mr. Zant is running late. What kind of secret handsome-guy shenanigans might he be up to? Haircut? Hair Club for Men? Handsome People Anonymous?

I'm sitting near the front, staring out the half-window, thinking these important questions. Right behind me is Maureen. I am not sure if she has any philosophy on seat-choosing, but maybe by moving to the second row instead of the first, she is taking one step away from nerd-dom and a tentative leap into the back rows of slackerhood.

I realize that there is a lot I don't know about Maureen Fields. And given the morbid thoughts I've been having, maybe I should get to know her better. Maybe we have something in common. Maybe a lot in common. She is giving off lots of signals to be left alone—scribbling in the black notebook and wearing her custom black earbuds with loud music blaring—but I still decide to talk to her. I see her flicking her phone with a lazy thumb, presumably changing songs. It seems like a better conversation-starter than asking about her philosophy of seat-choosing or the secret note-book, so I ask her about the music.

"What kind of music you got on there?" I say, super-friendly.

"What?" she says loudly, looking annoyed. I make the gesture that she should take off her earbuds.

"I said, whatcha listenin' to?" I flash the classic Langman smile. She still looks annoyed. It must be her. The Langman smile never fails.

"A bunch of bands you've probably never heard of," she says, all pissy.

"Just making conversation here," I say, holding my palms up in a gesture of mock surrender.

"Fine, it's the Sisters of Mercy," she says. "I'm sure you love them."

"Can't say I'm a particular fan of the SOM—but hey, I'm open to all music," I say.

"No one calls them the SOM," she says. I smile again. Then she stops and seems to look at me for the first time. Then she speaks, not to me, just near me. And about me. "Seriously, what does Guy Langman listen to?" she says. She is getting a *little* more involved in the conversation. I notice that she keeps one earbud in. Like she is only half-committed to the idea of talking to me. I mind, but I don't mind. That's how I live most of my life.

"All music is the same to me," I say. "I listen to whatever my mom is playing on the piano. Or whatever is on the radio. Or I listen to my dad's old records. I'm on a big Herb Alpert & the Tijuana Brass kick lately."

"Listening to old records had you briefly up here," she says, holding her hand high over her head. "Herb Alpert & the Tijuana

Brass . . ." She ever-so-slowly moves her hand down past her desk and leans over until it touches the dusty floor.

TK chimes in. "His theory is interesting, though," he says. "All music can be reduced to fundamental core similarities."

"Yeah," I say. "That's exactly what I was doing, expounding a theory about fundamental core whatever-the-hell-you-said."

He sniffs at me, still not looking up. TK's defining gesture. The sniff.

"Guy has no thoughts on anything," Maureen says to TK. Then she turns to me. "You can make fun of me for trying too hard, but you are just too lazy to look into what kind of music you like. You don't even take the steps to go beyond the records that already happen to be in your house? What are you saving all your energy for? You never do anything."

"All I was saying is that music is music—what's the difference?"

"And all I'm saying is that it's super-easy to sit there and make fun of everything like you're above the world, but you can't just refuse to take part in anything forever," she says. Seriously, why am I talking to her? Who is she—Anoop?

I try to change the subject. "I do know exactly what kind of movies I like," I say. She raises her eyebrows.

"Action," I say. "I can say with certainty that I like action movies."

"Figures," she says. Then she rolls her eyes, actually rolling one and then the other to make the point excessively clear. I had expected as much.

"Yeah, yeah," I say. "Action movies aren't something cool that someone smart is supposed to like, but I don't like them for the explosions and the violence. I like them for the dialogue."

"You watch action movies for the dialogue? That's like saying you read porno mags for the articles."

"My dad actually did read those articles. Or at least he claimed to . . ."

"Everybody claims to. Nobody does."

"Well, I do like the dialogue in action movies. Those dudes always know exactly what to say. I'm a big fan of the action-hero quip," I say.

"The action-hero quip?"

I look around the room for an example. "Like, I could take this chair and smash it over a bad guy's head and then be, like, 'Take a seat.'" I say it in a good action-hero growl. "Or I could stab somebody with this pencil and be, like, 'I think I've made my point.'"

To my surprise, Maureen laughs. "Those are really good!" she says. "What movies are those from?"

"I just made those up!" I say.

"No way!"

"I swear!"

"Pretty good," she says, nodding and smiling. "Do another one."

"How about if I smacked a villain with my book bag and said, 'Looks like you have some extra baggage.'"

"Not bad!" she says.

"You try one," I say.

"No, I couldn't," she says. "I suck at things like that. You're good. You should, like, write movies for a living!"

"Nah," I say. "Too much work. I saw an interview with a screenwriter and he was talking about how it takes like ten years to get your movie made, and then all these stupid film people just mess with it anyway, and—"

"You piss me off, Guy," Maureen says in a startling action-hero growl of her own. "I want to punch you so hard in the face."

"What the hell?" I say. "What brought that on? What did I do?"

"You have a gift and you won't pursue it because it's too much work? What the hell? Didn't you ever hear the expression 'Anything good requires effort'?"

"I heard it a little differently," I say. "My dad's version was, 'If you want your balls to shine, you got to use lots of wax' . . . I'm not sure that's the same thing, though, really. Maybe it was just a personal hygiene tip—"

Maureen shakes her head. It looks like maybe she is fighting a smile.

"Well, I am working on a book about my dad," I say. Why do I tell her this? What do I care what she thinks? *Let the schmucks say what they say, but in the end you're the one who has to look at your punim in the mirror every morning.* Another phrase of Dad's, which I once accidentally misquoted back to him as "You're the one who has to look at your *tuchus* in the mirror every morning," which is one odd morning ritual. *Punim* means "face." *Tuchus* means your rear end. You'd have to be flexible. More to the point: Why do I care what Maureen thinks? Am I trying to impress Maureen Fields?

"That's cool," she says. "Do you want that to be your job? You want to write books?"

"I don't know. That seems hard too. Why do we keep talking about my career goals? Who put you up to this? Anoop? My mother?"

"I think it's disturbing that it could equally be either," she says quietly. "Anoop is like a second mother to you. It's unhealthy."

"So who was it?" I ask Maureen.

"Neither! I'm just wondering. You seem so smart. What does the future hold for you? You need to figure it out ASAP."

Maureen says "ASAP" in a funny way. She doesn't spell it out. It's an acronym for "as soon as possible" so people usually say "A-S-A-P." She just said "a sap," like it was a thing. Anyway, I don't feel like giving her a real answer. So I give her a fake one. A sap.

"I heard about being a 'kept boy.' Maybe I could be a 'kept boy,'" I say.

"What the hell is that?" Maureen asks.

"Like you have some sugar momma and you lie around on the beach and just do it with her once in a while. I look good in a wet suit."

"You mean like a gigolo?"

"You don't get paid for the sex, she just keeps you around . . ."

"For the sex!"

"Yeah, I guess."

"That is the worst career goal I have ever heard," she says. I shrug. I don't tell her my other career goal, which is to be the guy who shovels the hippo crap at the zoo. I realize this is a weird goal, but I figure most every career is more or less shoveling hippo crap, so you might as well just go ahead and literally do it, you know? I'm deep.

Mr. Zant shows up finally, freshly waxed. Forensics Squad goes well, if uneventfully. More to the point, here's what happens next: Being Anoop-less means I don't have a ride home. I announce this to the group, and Maureen offers one with much excitement. OK, more like she just shrugs and mutters, "I guess we could, like, give you a ride or whatever." I know!

"Don't mind if I do," I say. "Do not mind if I do." We wait for Mrs. Fields and I try to picture her. When she shows up, Maureen's mom looks approximately exactly like the exact opposite of what I would have guessed. The chipper and tanned blond MILF behind the wheel of a midnight-black BMW is literally the very last person on earth I would have guessed would be the mother of Maureen Fields. Well, I suppose she could have been one of those tribeswomen from Social Studies class with the floppy pizza-dough boobs and whatever the female equivalent of the dong bracelet would be. I would have been slightly more surprised to see a topless tribeswoman introducing herself to me as Mrs. Fields, but honestly, only just slightly.

"Hello, Mrs. Fields," I manage to squeak out, trying to get into the car while holding my backpack over the embarrassing tent of my pants. Maureen rolls her eyes, then sullenly introduces me. "Ma, this is Guy. He needs a ride, okay?" She then shoves past me into the backseat. It seems rude to leave Mrs. Fields alone in the front, so I hop in next to her.

There is something so shocking and unavoidably sexy about Mrs. Fields that it is as though a naked model from a centerfold has come to life and offered to give me a ride home. I think about my dad's old *Playboys*. I imagine she is going to start telling me about her turn-ons and favorite ways to be kissed.

"Guy!" Maureen smacks me on the back of the head. "Wake the hell up!"

"Maureen," her mom says, her voice purring as smoothly as the car's well-tuned engine. "Watch that mouth of yours. I'm sure he just didn't hear the question."

"Yeah, I—I'm sorry, ma'am," I manage, using all the powers in my pubescent arsenal to keep my voice from cracking into a thousand pieces. Trying to sound cool. Trying to sound manly. "What was the question?"

"Where do you live, Guy?" Maureen spits at me. She is not nearly as kind as she was a few minutes ago. "What the hell do you think the question was? We don't know where you live." Then she mutters to herself, sort of talking to her balled-up fists. "Why the hell did we say we'd give him a ride? Why? Why? Why?"

"Oh, right," I say, ignoring the latter question. I notice Mrs. Fields's right hand poised over the touch-screen GPS in the car's dashboard. She wears several rings on her slender fingers, and her nails look freshly painted. Like her shoes, they are the color of blood.

I give her my address, then add, "It's the one at the end of the circle with the goofy sign that says 'Langman Manor.'"

"You are Guy *Langman*?" she says. I think I should probably not answer. I look at Maureen. She is somewhat less than helpful, giving me that big-eyed, head-shaking face that clearly means "I dunno, what the hell?"

Mrs. Fields continues, "Maureen talks about a Guy at home all the time, of course." I again look back at Maureen. She is shaking her head as if in vigorous disagreement with this statement. As if in vigorous disagreement with the whole world, maybe.

The black hood of her sweatshirt is pulled down so far over her eyes that it looks like the hoodie is trying to swallow her head. She looks like she is trying to shrink herself down to the size of a penny so that she can get lost like spare change between the cracks of the leather seats.

"I just never put it together," Mrs. Fields says. "Silly of me, really. I mean, how many Guys are there?" This is clearly a rhetorical question, yet for some reason I always answer rhetorical questions. It's, like, do I even know what "rhetorical" means? Don't answer that.

"Well, there was Sir Guy of Gisborne," I say. Smooth.

"I knew your family a long time ago," she says. "A lot of people thought it was, um, odd when your mom fell for Fran. Especially because he already had a son our age. Struck people as weird. Why would Tammy Reynolds fall for this old man? But not me. I always got it."

"Ew, Mom, stop crushing on Guy's dad," Maureen says.

"There was something about him, though," Mrs. Fields says. She takes her right hand off the wheel and clutches it to her chest. She grabs a bony protrusion of her collarbone. She holds her heart. Damn, Dad was a heartthrob. But wait.

"You knew my mom back then?" I say. "And, um, Dad's son?" What the hell?

"Sure," she says. "We both lived in Bayonne, then both ended up in Berry Ridge. Small world. Small state, anyway. I was so sorry to hear about your father's passing. He was the kind of man who was far too alive ever to die."

I can't let go of what she said earlier. This is amazing. Mrs. Fields knows about my half brother. The hum of the engine speaks to us like a soft whisper from another world. According to the GPS, we'll be at Langman Manor in about four minutes and I am just beginning to wrap my head around all this new information. And I'm hungry for more.

The digital clock on the GPS counts out its final minute. One minute to go. The LANGMAN MANOR sign is clearly in sight.

"Dad's son, his name is Steve, right?" I say, just making up a name, hoping she'll correct me.

"What? No," she says. "Your father named him Jacques. I'll never forget that. I'm surprised you didn't know that. Weird Jacques." She laughs. "Like Jacques Cousteau, the underwater diver person. That was a friend of your father's."

"Oh, right," I say, acting like I knew it all along. Amazing, how she fell into my trap. I do have good detective skills. *Muahahaha*. "Hey, so can we talk more about this sometime?" I say. It comes out wrong, like I am hitting on her. I'm not! But of course it looks that way. And okay, maybe I am. "I mean, I'm trying to write a book about my dad." It sounds stupid. I press on. Noble. Brave. Sir Guy of Goddamn Gisborne. "I'd love to hear some stories about what my parents were like back then."

She smiles, this heartstoppingly beautiful woman. Then she grabs her collarbone again. I can tell from her eyes that the shadows of a thousand nights are flashing across her brain.

"The past is the past, and only a fool will not let it be," she says as I get out of the car. Kinda poetic. I might have to write that down. Then I think she feels bad for calling me a fool. She smiles softly. "Just write this: 'Francis Langman was a hell of a man.'"

Then the beautiful car with the beautiful driver (and, oh yeah, also Maureen Fields) zooms away from the curb, leaving me in a small pile of grass clippings. I can't see into the tinted windows, but I am pretty sure Maureen is rolling her eyes in there, shaking her head in utter disapproval. Trying to disappear into the seat. Funny thing is, the thought makes me smile. Freaking Maureen Fields.

"Rules for Living": The Francis Langman Story
CHAPTER TWO

Francis Langman was a hell of a man.

CHAPTER THREE

And a liar.

CHAPTER ELEVEN

I walk into the house and see Mom apparently in a wrestling match with a vacuum cleaner. It is not going well. I'd say she was well on her way to defeat in the first round. Does wrestling have rounds? I'm not exactly what you'd call "into sports."

"Since when do you vacuum?" I ask. We always had a maid service. Mom looks up. Does she notice some bitterness in my voice? If so, she doesn't show it. "I was texting you. I needed a ride."

"I guess I didn't hear the phone. Did you know that vacuums are loud?"

"Um, yeah," I say.

"You know, we might have to curtail our spending around here. A lot of your father's money was in real estate or the stock market. Prices are going down, and . . ."

"Well, can you give me a ride to school tomorrow?" I ask, cutting her off.

"Didn't you hear what I said?" she asks.

"Yeah, sure, you're going to fire the maid. Can I have a ride tomorrow?"

"No," she says.

"No?"

"You heard me."

"I need a ride," I say.

She puts down the vacuum and looks at me seriously for the first time since I walked in.

"Is Anoop not going in again?" she says, narrowing her eyes at me.

"Diarrhea . . . ," I lie. Diarrhea is always a good lie, my friends. No one asks for details.

"Sorry to hear that," she says. "Probably all the curry. But I can't give you a ride. I have plans."

"What kind of plans?"

"I'm going into the city to see about selling one of Dad's New York properties," she says. "I have to leave ridiculously early."

"Can't you reschedule?"

"Can't you take the bus?"

"What?"

"Big yellow thing, maybe you've seen it around town. Its wheels go round and round. Round and round. Round and round."

"I am not taking the—"

"Let me finish," Mom says, holding up a hand. "All through the town." She does some jazz hands.

"Bus," I say.

"Why?" she asks, a little disappointed that I don't acknowledge the jazz hands. Normally I'm a pretty big fan of the jazz hands. I enjoy the old razzle-dazzle.

"The bus is like the last resort for the destitute and criminally insane."

"I rode the bus every day when I was in school."

"Well, it's not the 1940s anymore."

"I graduated in the 1980s," she says.

"Whatever. I'm not taking the bus. It's all freshmen and psychopaths, as if there's any difference. Am I right?" I can tell this fight is lost, so I am just getting obnoxious. I try to give Mom a high five. "Can a brother get an amen?!" I say.

"Guy, you're taking the bus," she says.

"Fine," I say, narrowing my eyes. I guess there is no way out of the bus. "But I get something in return." Life is a negotiation. Dad taught me that too.

"You're really going to sell one of Dad's properties?" I ask.

"I don't see any reason to hold on to it for, you know, sentimental reasons," she says. "We really could use the cash flow. Everything is losing value. Strange times."

"Strange times indeed," I say.

"I think I could live to be one hundred before I finish sorting through the paperwork in his, you know . . ." Here she lets her voice fall away.

Mom could never bring herself to say the word "will." Never once. She could make a million and one jokes about Dad and say "dead" with no problem. But she refuses to say "will" in that context. I think I understand why. It makes the whole thing seem like a business transaction. She always worried that people thought she married him for his money, and she was very touchy about it.

Dad's death is still a shock to her, I think. How could it not have been? Just another day of Fran playing dead in his armchair. She came down to see him, to play the stupid game. She sat on his lap, she told me. She kissed him. And he was cold. And she knew. She knew.

Should I tell Mom what Mrs. Fields said? How can I? How can I not? But I need to know more.

"Tell me . . . tell me more about him," I say. "About when he was young."

"I really don't think I know much more than you, Guy," she says. "So much of that happened before I was around."

"Come on, Mom," I say. "How did a Jewish kid from Newark end up scuba-diving with Jacques Cousteau in the first place?"

"Oh, I don't know. That was your father, though. If he met someone once, they loved him forever. He went on a trip to the islands when he was young, and Jacques was there and somehow your father talked his way onto his boat. He could talk his way through a locked vault, your father."

Sometimes I hate my mom. I really do. *She* is a locked vault. Is she ever going to talk about anything real? How can your husband die and you just joke about it? Doesn't she realize that it's messing me up to never get it all out there? Of course I say none of this. The favor I ask for in return? Tacos from Taco City for dinner. Maybe I should have held out for something greater, but sometimes it's the little things. After we eat, I go up to my room and write some more:

"Rules for Living": The Francis Langman Story
CHAPTER FOUR

> *"You must respect everyone you meet, yet fear no one you meet. No matter who they are, they don't know what the hell they're doing in this life any more than you do." —Francis Langman*

> *Francis Langman was on a trip to the islands when he met Jacques Cousteau, the French seaman who made all those movies. Now that the author*

considers it, Fran probably cracked the ice with
J. Cousteau with some sort of "seaman" joke. He
probably bumped into him and then said, "Aw,
man. Now I got seaman all over me." That's what
the author would have done.

Langman then talked his way into the
Cousteaus' inner circle and began taking scuba
seriously. He used his knowledge of bagel-making to
help with some sort of scuba valve. Bagels are boiled
in a vat, and there are a lot of valves and tubes.
It's oddly rather like scuba—just with more cream
cheese and less sharks. Both have a fair amount of
tuna, I guess.

Anyway, he invented the Langman valve. It's
still out there. You can look that up. It's part of
most every scuba system sold in the past thirty
years. But the real money came from the treasure.
It was a sunken boat from the 1600s. He kept some
of it, sold some. He had a few ancient coins in the
attic, supposedly worth a ton. He always told me
never to tell anyone about them. Probably they are
cursed.

The next step was taking that money and
buying real estate and stock. Which was cool for a
long time, because property makes money without
doing anything. "Property owner" is really a sweet
lazy man's game. But it sucks now, because Mom
has to sell some of the properties. The main reason
this sucks is because the author needs a ride to school
tomorrow, and now he has to ride the stupid bus.

Why doesn't Mom deal with her grief? Why does the global real estate market have to collapse the one day I need a ride? Why did Dad have to die, anyway? I'm not saying the whole world is against me, but sometimes I really think it just might be.

What is up with Jacques Langman? Psycho. What was he doing at the funeral? What is his angle? Where is he living? Can I use my bad-ass forensics skills to find him? And what do I say to him when I do?

I fear this book is losing some of its literary objectivity. It's just becoming Guy Langman's Sad Journal, but I'm not keeping a feelings journal because you told me to, Dr. Waters. I'm not!

CHAPTER TWELVE

The population of bus-riding students at Berry Ridge High is ridiculously small. Absolutely every student of driving age not named for Sir Guy of Goddamn Gisborne has a car and drives themselves. And everyone who is too young to drive hitches a ride from someone else in class or gets their parents to drive them. I think the parents like showing off in the parking lot even if they pretend they don't like having to haul their kids in. The parking lot is like some sort of luxury car show.

I walk down to the bus stop in the gray half-light of a wet morning. I wonder if the bus driver will even notice me here. There is never anyone at this stop, as far as I know. I haven't taken the bus in years, and at first I couldn't even remember where the bus stop is. Mom assured me that it's in the same old place that it ever was—on the corner near the playground, across from Mrs. Martin's huge white house with the pillars. Standing there in the shadow of that big house, staring at the towering maple trees—it brings back innocent memories of elementary school.

The whole world seemed brighter back then. Cleaner too. Maybe the bus won't stop. What would I do with my day? Just stand here. Maybe a nap on the bench. Maybe go down the slide a few hundred times. That's all it took back then to feel joy. Amazing. Climb up, whoosh down. A slide—the sheer basic existence of gravity—was enough to fill your elementary-school-aged heart with glee. Shit is, to put it mildly, quite a bit more complicated these days. I spent a lot of time imagining the awesomeness of "being a teenager" when I was in elementary school. I thought it would be all parties and fast cars and hot girls. I thought I'd wear tank tops and jeans and lean against a car and that would be it. I even thought it would be great when I was old enough so that my parents would let me mow the lawn. Ha. Irony. Nothing is ever what we think it will be. That's why I can't get a boner about college—it's just going to be more of the same stupid crap. I see the bus approach through my nostalgic haze and, unfortunately, it stops. Doesn't even look surprised to see me. Mom probably called ahead. She would.

I enter the bus, sizing up the pleasant and plump middle-aged lady bouncing behind the wheel. She's wearing a sweatshirt with a picture of a cat wrapped in red yarn. Even the curls of her hair appear to be smiling. "Good morning!" she sings, the tune a chipper riff on the first three notes of "Jingle Bells."

I narrow my eyes. "I'm onto you," I say. She laughs. "I'm not kidding," I say. She laughs again. With some people, you just can't win.

I scan the bus. It is a ridiculous waste of gasoline with its enormous rattling engine and one hundred seats. Only a few seats are occupied. There are a couple of freshmen whose names I don't know and one kid from my grade sitting alone.

"Hey, Hairston," I say. Who else but Hairston Danforth III? Penis-Head glumly blinks a weary hello. His black hair is uncombed, a messy pile of bed head. He runs his fingers through it while staring at me, then returns his eyes to the screen of his smartphone. Who knows what he's doing on there. Rumor has it that Hairston is some sort of hacker. A genius at it. I'm not sure I believe that. There have been lots of weird rumors about Hairston since he moved into town a few years back. That he's a millionaire. That he's a heroin addict. A kleptomaniac. An arms smuggler. That he takes off his glasses and becomes a crime-fighting caped crusader. Okay, not really that last one.

I think he's just a lonely guy who likes farting around with computers and stuff because it's easier than talking to people. Hairston is often dressed in a peculiar fashion, and this day is no exception. He is wearing a sweater with dancing reindeer on it. Does he shop at the same place as the bus driver? Probably. "You ride the bus?" I ask. It is a dumb question. What tipped me off? The fact that he is riding on the bus?

"Indeed, it would seem that I do," he says. His voice matches his face. It is a dirge, a sad funeral march. For some reason, whenever anyone talks to me in that sad, slow way I get increasingly and annoyingly chipper. My attempt to balance out the yin and yang of the universe, I guess.

"Why's that, Harry?" I ask, taking the seat in front of him and tapping happily on the plastic seat.

"My parents are out of town," he says, with no trace of joy. "They are quite often out of town. Business trips and the like."

He is making it clear that he wishes not to continue this conversation. His eyes head back down to the screen of his phone. His voice has the sound of a door being locked behind you. I press on, driven by some inner need to be annoying, I guess.

"So the parents are away on business, huh, Hair-Bear?" I ask. "What kind of business are they in?"

"The family business," he says. "The business of business of business."

This makes no sense, but I let it go. I just keep babbling. I don't know why. "My dad got rich doing sea-diving and stuff. He has literal sunken treasure in our house. Coins and stuff in a cigar box in the attic. Crazy, right?" He shrugs. I press on, changing the topic just to keep talking, I guess. "You don't have your own car?" I ask. "You're a junior, right? You should be driving fast, wearing a tank top and jeans."

"I'm only fifteen," he says, blinking his sad eyes.

"Wait, what? How did you end up as a fifteen-year-old junior?" I ask.

He looks up. His face shows nothing, a dull mask. He doesn't even blink as we stare at each other for an awkwardly long time. I think I see his right eyebrow twitch, but that might just be in my mind. It's a pretty impressive set of eyebrows he has. It really looks like they should have a heartbeat of their own.

"Go on," I say.

"Must I?" he asks.

"Yes," I say. I have no authority to demand that he go on, but acting like you have authority in any situation usually works. I'd seen Dad do it a million times. Never felt like I could try it myself. Thing is, though, it actually works. On Penis-Head, anyway.

"When I was in second grade, all the other kids teased me mercilessly," Hairston says.

"The Penis-Head thing?" I ask. He gives me a startled look, drawing his arms in toward his chest quickly.

"No!"

"Oh. Sorry."

"Do people call me Penis-Head?" he asks.

"You know that they do," I say. "I mean, some people. Jerks, mostly."

"Yeah, I know they do," he says. "I was just joking. You do. You call me that."

"Yeah, but I'm not a jerk. I'm just breaking your balls, Harry. It's not your fault you can't eat peanuts. Hey, look at me, I hate ketchup."

"Well, I wish that you would not, ahem, break my balls . . . And please don't call me Harry. I hate that worse than Penis-Head."

"Really? Do I really need to call you Hairston Danforth the Third all the time?"

"Just Hairston is fine."

"So, Just Hairston, what happened back in second grade?"

"Just general teasing, I guess. The standard schoolyard torment that has become the fundamental architecture of my life." Hairston talks exactly like an old man when you get him talking. It is kinda weird. Especially for a fifteen-year-old.

"Kids are jerks," I say, not knowing what else to say.

He sighs, closing his puffy eyes, a gesture full of pain and too much world-weariness for someone so young. I decide to be nicer to Penis—Hairston—from now on.

"The kids, they were mean," he says. I guess we're not done here. "I convinced my mother to lobby the school to let me skip a grade."

"Ah, I see," I say. "She wrote a check, like with the peanut thing, and they let you skip to third grade?"

"Something like that," he says. "Oh, okay, exactly that."

"Did it work out for ya?" I ask.

"How's that?"

"Was the third-grade experience more to your liking?" I decide to try to make myself talk like an old man to see if he can better understand me.

"What do you think the third-grade experience was like for me?" he asks, again with the world-weary sigh.

"I'm going to go out on a limb and say that the third graders were just as big of jerks as the second graders."

"Even bigger."

"Sorry to hear that," I say. Thing is, I *am* sorry to hear it.

"Which is why I'm on the bus. Parents are out of town. I won't be sixteen until the end of the year. I have friends, but they all go to North Berry Ridge."

"Stupid North Berry Ridge," I say reflexively.

"None of our classmates is exactly dying to show up at school carting old Penis-Head around."

I almost feel like I should offer him a ride sometime. But it's Anoop's call, I guess. All I say is, "Sucks."

"The sooner I'm out of here, the better," he says. He gestures toward the mostly empty bus, but I'm pretty sure he doesn't just mean the bus. "For everyone."

"And the sooner you can get into that family business," I say, ignoring that final low-self-esteem comment and trying to encourage Hairston to be happy.

"The business of business," he says, "does not interest me."

What does interest him? I don't ask. Do I want to know? Not really. "Hey, you should come back to Forensics! It's pretty fun." Why do I say that? Do I even think it?

"I do enjoy Forensics," he says. "But I decided I did not wish to belong to any club which would have me as a member."

"Groucho Marx!" I say. "One of my dad's favorites."

"Plus it cut into the time I reserve for my hobbies."

"Okay, sure," I say. "Stamp-collecting, stuff like that?"

"Something like that," he says with an evil grin. Then he changes the subject. "Hey, sorry about your dad," Hairston says. The bus swings to a stop outside of school. I am glad I don't have to think too much about how to respond to that.

"Okay, see you later, dude!" I blurt. I make my way past the empty rows. "School-bus lady," I say. "I'm onto you."

"Have a great day," she sings like it's the final refrain of a great Broadway show tune.

"I'm onto you," I say.

CHAPTER THIRTEEN

Being Anoop-less, my day is lonely. Here's there, but he's not there. It's especially bad at lunch. Where is he? I look around. Just, you know, taking in the sights. Enjoying the institutional orange-colored walls and the view of the parking lot. Shut up, I'm not looking for Anoop. I don't care where he is. I think about trying to find Hairston, of all people, just to have someone to shoot the breeze with, but even he is nowhere to be found. It's a weird feeling, the sensation that everyone in the world is avoiding you. The cafeteria is filled with a thousand little dramas, fights and teasing and studying and obsessive panic over stuff that pretty clearly doesn't mean anything. Everyone is fixing their hair all the time. For what? I feel deep with these kinds of thoughts as I sit alone eating my pesto and leeks (or whatever).

More deep thoughts: Maybe someday I'll leave all the nonsense of life behind and go live on top of a mountain. What did Dad say about that, though? "People who try to escape life are really just trying to escape their own minds. Which is unfortunate because of how it's strapped inside your head." Something like that. True enough. Plus, mountains are really high up there. Not a big fan of climbing. And no matter where you are, you still have to look at your *tuchus* in the mirror every morning. I pass through the rest of the day having thoughts like this. Trying to focus on literature, failing. Trying to care about Social Studies, failing. Trying to pretend I'm a real person living a real life. Failing.

I do go to Forensics Squad after school. As soon as I enter the dungeon, the mood feels strange. No Anoop. I am wondering if Maureen will be cool toward me like she was when she offered a ride or totally weird to me like she was in the car. Was it her mom who made her act weird? Did people hear that I invited Penis-Head to come back? What if he shows up?

Maureen Fields walks in. She catches my eye. No, not like that. It's her outfit. She has on black and gray camouflage-patterned pants and a black army-style jacket studded with bright silver points up and down the collar. It gives her the look of a soldier with rounds of bullets strapped to her chest. Her books are crammed into an army surplus backpack that has been turned nearly black with scrawlings from what must have been a whole case of black markers. The only part of her outfit with any touch of color is her hair—the bangs of which have been bleached and then died a shocking pink. You wouldn't dress like that unless you wanted people to comment on it, right? One would think. One would be wrong.

"Hey, MF, nice look," I say. She scowls. I can see her jaw muscles working. She is literally grinding her teeth at me. "I did not ask for your approval, Guy," she says.

"Dude, I'm just saying I like it."

"Don't call me dude."

"What the hell?" I ask. "What did I say?"

"I know you're going to make fun of me, and I'm not in the mood to hear it. I could make fun of your outfit if I wanted to."

I am wearing the standard GL ensemble, the most classic outfit the world has ever known: white T-shirt, jeans, and Chuck Taylor sneakers.

"I don't want you to make fun of me, no. But I also feel

like pointing out that I'm dressed in a way that is beyond reproach."

"Beyond reproach?"

"Beyond reproach."

"Your shoes are untied."

"Why tie them? They're just going to have to be untied again anyway."

"That's like saying 'Why breathe in? You have to breathe out eventually.'"

"Exactly."

"So why live at all? Why even bother existing if you're just going to coast through, doing as little as possible? Why be just another sheep to the slaughter, another cog in the wheel, another boring asshole in jeans and a T-shirt?"

"I may be an asshole, but I am not boring."

"I don't know why I even bother talking to you, ever. Consider this our last chat." She takes out a pen and starts writing.

The idea of Maureen not talking to me bothers me a little bit for a reason I can't place. I decide to reach out a little.

"Hey, I'm sorry. Listen. Can I tell you a secret?"

She keeps her arms folded and her eyes narrowed, but I see a hint of a smile at the edges of her mouth. No one can resist a secret.

"You better not be messing with me," she says.

"Totally serious," I say. She uncrosses her arms. I continue. "I know they are pretty ridiculous, but damn, I sort of want to start wearing ascots."

"What?"

"Ascots. Like scarves. My dad used to wear one."

Her mouth opens widely and her eyes light up. She is like a whole new Maureen all of a sudden.

"What did I say?"

"I love ascots!" she says.

"Are you breaking my balls? I know ascots are pretty dumb, but—"

"No, I mean, yes, but that's why they're awesome. I really think you should start wearing an ascot."

"Maybe I will, someday," I say. "Someday I will."

I have a hard time picturing myself making good on the promise, but the thought makes me smile. Is there any reason you can't show up at high school wearing an ascot? Not really.

Now it's Forensics Time, MFs! Mr. Zant scheduled an extra session this week for a "very special" lesson. I can barely contain my excitement. Mr. Zant walks in with a laptop under his arm. "Can anyone guess what we'll be doing today?" he asks the group. What's left of us, anyway. So weird that I outlasted Anoop.

"I'm gonna go out on a limb here and say we're doing some computer forensics," TK says. "Call me crazy."

"You *are* crazy," Mr. Zant says. Then he does that thing where he cocks his head sideways and freezes his mouth into an eerie smile. He holds it for seriously a minute or longer, which might not seem that long, but is pretty insane to see in person. Then he shakes it off and resumes talking. "You are close, T-to-the-K," he says. "But in fact today's forensics lesson is specifically on fractography."

Maureen looks really pleased. Big fractography fan over here, I guess. While Zant talks—okay, it's sort of cool that fractography is "the way things break"—I think about Maureen and how she seems like she hates me, but then maybe not? Why does she know about fractography? Does she read books on forensics for fun? And should I really start wearing an ascot? And then, yeah, I go back to thinking about Raquel and Anoop. Should I just be happy for them? It's so weird. Looking at the two of them, you'd imagine that she probably wouldn't let him sniff her bra if he was the last guy on earth. Wait: Why would he even want to sniff her bra? Do I want to? Kinda. And why does the thought give me a boner? And why does Mr. Zant call on me right as I am sprouting a healthy wood?

"Could you repeat the question, Mr. Z?" I ask. My voice is about four octaves too high on the word "you," and the word "question" comes out like "quest-ee-own" for some reason. I'm so pathetic.

"Just asking if you'd like to come up to get a better look at the screen like the rest of us," he says. I hadn't noticed that everyone else had gotten out of their seats and was gathered around Mr. Z's laptop. He is showing close-up images of two broken bottles. He is explaining how you can tell that one was broken by severe force, while the other was dropped to the ground. All that just from some broken glass. It caught a murderer too. I kinda *do* want to see it. If I weren't having this, um, situation. In my pants.

"I'm just going to stay here, if that's cool," I say, trying to sound, well, cool. Probably failing.

"Are you sure?" he asks.

"Yeah, sounds fascinating," I say. "But I'm just gonna chill back here for a bit."

"Are you sure?" he asks. "Really sure?"

"Yes!" I yell.

Now I'm just going to go ahead and put this out there as a general public-service announcement if any teachers happen to be reading this. If a guy (or Guy) in your high school class is acting weird about standing up for some reason, and is making excuses for not coming to the board or coming over to see your laptop or whatever, the reason is clear. He has a boner. Please do not make him get up. It's cruel. Thank you. This has been a public-service announcement brought to you by Guy Langman, Inc.

"Suit yourself," he says. I say nothing more, choosing to quit while I am behind. Brilliant! It is actually kind of interesting, the whole fractography thing, from what I can tell safely in the boner zone in the back.

"It's kinda poetic, the whole idea," Maureen says. "The way things break. Everything breaks, it's just a matter of how."

"Poetic. I never thought of it that way," Zant says.

Raquel rolls her eyes. She thinks she can be above everything just by being beautiful. It's sort of annoying, really. Anoop can freaking have her.

Mr. Zant says, "We're going to sort of take it easy for a while—Guy, I know this will be a challenge for you." I manage a weak smile while everyone laughs. "Don't forget to mark your calendars for our big final project. Hopefully the weather will be good and we'll do the simulated scene in the field. I'll plant the evidence. You'll solve the crime."

"Oh, I'll solve it," I say. "I'll solve it indeed." Why do I say that? No idea.

But before diving into that crime, I have some of my own research to do.

I take the "activity bus" home, which is even more sparsely populated than the morning bus. It's just me and the creepy bus driver on the creepy short bus. I'm starting to seriously think about studying for that driver's license. On the ride, I have basically one thought: How to find Jacques Langman? I feel proud of myself for landing the name, but I don't know what to do with it. Would Mom be helpful? It's not like I asked. She doesn't even know I got as far as finding the name. And okay, I'm having two thoughts: How can I find Jacques Langman, and *should* I find Jacques Langman? Is there a reason he was kept secret from me? Probably. But wouldn't it be nice to talk to my own freaking brother? Could anyone else on earth know what the loss of Fran is like? Maybe it would help. Closure. That's a Dr. Waters word.

The bus drops me off, and I wander up the long, winding driveway. The trees are looking overgrown. A rainspout blew off the house in a storm a few weeks ago and is still sitting in the grass. Is that something I'm supposed to take care of now? Are we going to move? It's crazy how these little things make me think of Dad.

When I get to the door, I see another little bit of life that hasn't been taken care of—a phone book was delivered and never brought in. The phone book seems like such a useless thing in today's world. Who uses a phone book these days? It can sit out there, rotting forever, for all I care. But then, hey, I have a thought. What if Jacques Langman lives nearby? Would his number be listed in there? Could it be that easy?

I lift the book out of the bag. It's a little wet, but I can still read it okay. I flip through and find the "L's." And oh man, the only Langman in the phone book is Francis. Pretty weird, seeing it there. The name and number of a dead man. You never think about stuff like that. Should we notify someone? I flip through the pages, wondering, How many dead people are in the phone book? Weird thought. I scan the names. Every one of them will die someday. This giant, hefty book. Corpses all, one day. Nice. Obsessive thoughts of death are a major sign of depression, says Dr. Waters. Maybe obsessive thoughts of death are just a sign that you're paying attention to life.

I scan the pages, not looking for anything in particular. Then I see someone whose last name is "Boner" and I laugh out loud. Frank Boner. There are actually a whole clan of them. Steve Boner, Jill Boner. A whole crew of Boners. Family reunions must be a trip. What do you call a group of Boners? Is there a word for it? A flock of Boners? Sounds right. I had a flock of boners in Forensics today.

I flip through the book a bit more and another thought crosses my mind. Hairston Danforth. Maybe I could look up Penis-Head and see if he could help me locate Jacques. If it's true that he's got hacker skills, maybe he knows where to find stuff like that. He could snoop around somehow and figure things out. I'm a good snoop myself, and I have the number within seconds. Okay, it's right there in black and white, hardly a secret. His father's name is also Hairston, of course, so under DANFORTH, HAIRSTON, a number is listed. I unlock the door of Langman Manor and head into the house. I find myself pressing the numbers on the alarm, but there's no reason to disarm it. Mom never remembers to set it, and neither do I. But I still find myself disarming it, as if Dad were still here. I find it easy to see why people believe in ghosts.

I toss the phone book onto the granite countertop, pick up

the phone, and dial the number for the Danforth residence. Sure enough, Penis-Head picks up.

"Hey, Hairston," I say. "Frank Boner here." I don't know why I say it. He says nothing. It sounds like he's about to hang up. I don't want to lose my chance, so I quickly yell, "J/K! It's Guy Langman from school. How's it going?"

"It is going fine," he says. His voice is flat. If he's surprised that I'm calling, he doesn't show it. "I thought you were another prank phone call."

"Oh, I'm sorry," I said. "I just saw some guy named Frank Boner in the phone book when I was looking up your number. It made me laugh."

"Ha," he says. Then, "Why were you looking me up in the phone book?"

"There was one sitting on the deck. I know I could have looked you up online or whatever . . ."

"No," he says. "I mean, why were you looking for *my* number?"

"Well, Hair-Bear," I say. "I have a favor to ask of you."

"Okay," he says. "Don't call me that."

"Sure. Well, is it true that you have mad computer skillz?"

"Mad skills?"

"With a 'z.' You have to say it like that. Mad skillzzzzzz."

"Um, what?"

"Whatever. I mean, like you're good at doing computer stuff."

"I guess so. Let me guess: you got a virus downloading porn?"

"No, it's just—" I start to explain, but he cuts me off.

"You want some codes to hack the pay-porn sites?"

"Nah, I'm—"

"You need more storage to save your porn?"

"Hairston," I say loudly. "Everyone knows I prefer my porn analog. This is about something else."

"Analog porn, huh?"

I sigh. "My dad left behind a treasure trove of old *Playboys*. I know those chicks are like sixty now, which is weird, but who cares, right? Way hotter than any girl out there today."

"Yeah, I guess."

"I'll give you one if you want. You strike me as a Lisa Baker kind of dude. She was 1967 Playmate of the Year and well deserving of the honor. It will pain me to part with her, I'll tell you that much."

"Why are you being so nice to me?"

"I need a favor. I need to find someone."

"Okay, and you think I can help?" he asks, maybe just the tiniest bit of cheer creeping into his voice.

"Yeah, can't you hack into some databases or something?"

"I don't know. Maybe. What do you know?"

I tell Hairston what I know about Jacques Langman—his name, his approximate age. He seems a bit less interested now that we're not talking about porn, but he grunts in assent when I'm done with my spiel.

"Do you want to hold?" he says.

"You're going to do it right now?" I ask.

"Sure," he says. "I have my laptop right here. It's not like it's hacking. It's just rummaging around through some government records, cross-searching phone directories. It's on the open Web. No big deal. I'll figure it out."

"It's pretty creepy how good you are at that," I say. "You'd make a good cop."

"I guess," he says.

"Or a criminal."

"Thanks?" he laughs. I laugh. Laughing it up with Penis-Head. I hear the clacking of the keys on his laptop. He whistles a little tune. I go to the fridge and look for something good. There isn't anything, so I just chug some milk out of the bottle. And a few moments later he has it. "Jacques Langman," he says. "There's only one in the country. He was arrested in Pennsylvania about twenty years ago."

"For what?" I spit the milk out. It splashes a white puddle onto the black counter. It looks like the chalk outline of a corpse. I feel sick to my stomach.

"Murder," he says.

"What?" I shriek.

"Just kidding, dude. Relax."

"Oh man, why did you say that?" I yell. I feel my heart slowly crawl back to the approximate region of my chest where it belongs.

"It was actually just assault with a deadly weapon," he says.

"Very funny," I say.

"No, that part is serious. He really was arrested for assault with a deadly weapon for attacking a cop in Easton, Pennsylvania."

"That's a pretty freaking weird joke, Hairston."

"Whatever. He got off." I hear some more keys clacking.

"Whoa. Where is he now?"

"Hold on. Let me check this other thing and . . . It seems like he lives in New York. Last updated address is Manhattan. Not too far from here at all." He reads the address and I scramble to find a pen to write it down. I scribble it into the margin of the DANFORTH page of the phone book, though I'm not quite sure why.

"Hello?" Hairston says.

"Yeah, I'm still here," I say.

"You going to tell me why you need this particular piece of information?" he asks.

"Not really," I say.

"You going to at least say 'Thank you, Hairston, for being so awesome' or something?" he says.

"Thank you, Hairston, for being so, so awesome," I say, aware that my voice sounds insincere. I do mean it, though. I do appreciate it. It's just hard to focus, staring at the address of Jacques Langman written in black ink in the margins of a phone book.

"I'll take that *Playboy* at school. Lisa Baker. In a brown paper bag, please."

"Sure, sure," I say, totally distracted. Now that I have the means to do it, I'm not so sure I should try to find Jacques Langman anymore. Trouble is, what if he tries to find me?

I decide to do some more writing on the book, but it's pretty much falling apart. I keep trying to pretend I'm an objective biographer, and I don't think you're supposed to say "I" in that kind of reporting, so I keep saying "the author." It just sounds weird and eventually it's just me writing about myself. But not because you told me to, Dr. Waters!

"Rules for Living": The Francis Langman Story
CHAPTER FIVE

> *"Do not trust those who love death or those who hide from it. Death is part of life, but so is the clap. And let me tell you: it is no fun, but you'd be foolish to pretend it doesn't exist. Seriously, Guy, wear a rubber."* —Francis Langman

When Dad died, the author went through a fast-forward version of those five stages of grief. He didn't realize it at the time, but thank the Lord for Dr. Waters. She told him there'd be denial, anger, bargaining, depression, and acceptance. "Not for me, there won't," the author said. That was denial? But what he meant was that there wouldn't be acceptance. And really, there hasn't been. The author refuses to admit that Francis is gone. Suck on that, fifth stage.

But wait, what does that mean, that the author refuses to accept it? That he'll be stuck in the depression stage forever? To be honest, sometimes the author thinks that is where he is and will always be. Sure, he likes to joke around, but what if that is just hiding his sadness? What if the comedy is just a way to swallow the tragedy? The tragedy that is life. And what if Anoop is right? What if the reason I don't care about college, about life, about anything, is just because I'm depressed? Well, who wouldn't be? Life is depressing. Shit.

CHAPTER FOURTEEN

Every once in a while Mom gets the idea that she should cook. It's usually a bad idea. It's not that she's a terrible cook, it's just that if you're a fan of *human* food, you might want to consider takeout. Ha-ha, that's something Dad used to say. Anyway, Mom makes some sort of weird chicken dish tonight, and it's chewy and quite unpleasant. I'm sort of glad it's chewy, though, so I can act as though my mouth is just very busy and there's no way I can possibly talk. Because she is in a talking mood. Maybe it's the wine. I'm just not in the mood to care. I don't want to care about how her day was. I don't want to care about the property she's selling. I don't want to care about any of it. My mind is on Jacques Langman and I almost mention it a dozen times. But each time I just shove another piece of chewy chicken into my mouth and keep the Jacques-talk to myself. It doesn't seem like anything good would come from sharing. At least not until I know a little more.

I spend a mind-numbing night watching TV. It's some reality show about teen moms who live in a renovated house and learn to become chefs while kickboxing. Or something. I am not really paying attention. It's okay having your mind numbed sometimes, right? Well, maybe it would be if it actually worked. I just feel restless. I head to bed on the early side, trying not to think about how big and empty the house feels. I push open the door to my bedroom, an act that becomes more difficult by the day due to the growing mountain of dirty clothes on the floor. I flop into bed and fall asleep. Just as I reach a blissful state of snoozing, I'm gently woken up by a horrible scream.

"Fran!" The voice is coming from my mom's room, of course, echoing down the hall. Is she dreaming? Seeing a ghost? I try to ignore it. Then I hear a thump. What the hell? Maybe there really is a ghost. This time Mom says my name.

"Guy!" She sounds panicked.

"What?" I say. Actually I half whisper, half scream it.

"Come here," she says.

"You come *here*," I hiss. Then I realize that's not a very manly thing to say, so I get up and go down the hall to her room. I half open the door and stick my head in. The huge bed in the middle of the room is barely visible.

"Did you hear that?" she asks.

"I heard you talking to Dad," I say. "I don't think he's going to answer."

"No, not that," she says. "That was just reflex. I heard a noise and yelled his name."

"You heard a noise?

"Up in the attic, I think."

"You're crazy," I say, even though I too heard a thump. Then it comes again. Louder. Not just a thump, but a voice. It seems to be saying "Crap."

Mom jumps out of bed and grabs me. We stand there like that, frozen in the mostly dark room, paralyzed with fear.

"Intruder!" she says. "Where's the phone?"

"I don't know," I say, annoyed. She turns a light on and we look for a phone. The cordless isn't in the room. One of us has to go back down the hall to my room to retrieve my cell. My instinct is to vote for Mom to do it. But I know that's not right. So I volunteer myself, even though the words feel weird coming out of my mouth. "I'll do it." Who is that talking? My heart is racing, and I'm sweating, and for some reason I feel like I really have to go to the bathroom. I inch my way down the hall, taking tiny steps. I adopt a karate stance even though I don't really know anything about karate. I mean, sure, I took lessons at the Berry Ridge Mall for about six weeks when I was nine, but I didn't quite achieve the rank of black belt. Not even a white belt, which is the belt they start you with. I don't think I got any belt at all. Not even a pair of suspenders. Watch out for my fists of fury.

I sneak back into my room and look for my phone. Why is this place such a mess? I sort of wish that it wasn't filled with laundry and junk. I know my phone is in a pants pocket, but which pants? Why do I have so many pants? Why do we have to have so many pants in a world where intruders are in your attic? Finally I locate the phone and rush back down the hall, holding it like a lance. Mom has apparently been looking for household items to use as a weapon and has settled on the ever-lethal combo of a jewelry box and a curling iron. Yeah, that'll work if we need to give him a makeover.

"I think he's gone," she says, hopeful. "But I'm going upstairs to check."

"No you're not!" I say. The force of my words seems to surprise her.

"At least let me call," she says. I hand her the phone and she dials 911. She tells the dispatcher that we have an intruder, gives our address and some other information, and hangs up. The more

I hear the word "intruder," the less it sounds like a real word. Intruder. Intruder. Intruder. There is an intruder in my life. Within minutes, two members of the Berry Ridge Police Department are at our door. They both have flashlights and guns and mustaches blazing. Mom shows them the door to the attic, and they creep up the steps. They motion that we should get out of the house, so we do. We're standing there in the night, wearing pajamas. Then Mom starts to cry. That's not very Mom-like. I put my arm around her. She cries harder.

After a few minutes the two police officers meet us outside. They tell us that the house is clear. "All clear," they say in their jargon. "He must have left the way he came," they say. Well, one of them says it. They don't talk in unison. It's mainly the older one talking. But he says it like maybe he doesn't really believe us that anyone was there in the first place, which is highly annoying. We *heard* something—wind doesn't mutter "Crap." So the police take a bunch of information from us, as if filling out a stupid report is supposed to make us feel better. If a killer is standing over you with a knife, he'll really check to see if you filled out some paperwork. Sorry, sir, I know you want to slit my throat, but if you check at police headquarters, you will notice that I have all the correct paperwork.

"Want to have a look?" the older of the two says. "See if you notice anything missing."

The older one has holstered his flashlight, but he hasn't turned it off, so it makes a bright spotlight on his left foot. Like his foot is onstage, about to launch into a song.

"Will you . . . come with us?" Mom asks. She's so scared. It breaks my heart. They follow us up. Mom and I both notice at once. The cigar box. Dad's coins. Gone. Mom starts to cry. I try to explain to the police. They look perplexed.

"Anything else you'd like me to note?" the younger officer asks. My gaze returns to his eyes. His pencil is poised over his small notebook. He looks like a waiter asking what type of soup I want. I'm tempted to blurt out, "I'll have the beef orzo." Also, I'd like him to note that this whole thing would be a hell of a lot easier to handle if Dad were here. Please put that in your report, Officer. Note that life isn't fair.

Of course I don't say that. Instead, I mumble, "Nothing." I think Mom is thinking the same thing—about Dad, that is, not about beef orzo. The corners of her mouth start to tremble and her hands are balled into tight fists.

"Let's go downstairs, Guy," she says. She's giving up. I think, What would Fran do? And yeah, he'd probably make some dumb joke or two, but he'd probably also take charge.

"Are you guys in a rush?" I ask the now startled-looking cops. "Do some analysis. Let's get some fingerprints, look for DNA, stuff like that." The policemen look at each other and sort of smirk. It pisses me off. "Listen," I say. "I'm not as dumb as you think I am. I don't just watch forensics shows on TV. I learned all about this in school. And I know what you're going to say. You're going to say this was a nonviolent crime, and that the way this shit goes down is nothing like on TV."

Mom looks shocked that I said "shit" to a police officer. As if they haven't heard worse. I continue.

"I'm telling you, we're lucky. This might not have been a violent crime this time, but maybe it will be next time. Let's stop this freak before things get really bad here." They look at me with a little more respect. But they aren't exactly calling in the pros. They think my imagination is just getting the best of me. I know that isn't true, but I also know I can't change their minds. The Berry Ridge Police Department forensics team isn't coming. There is only one thing to do. I have to take charge. I have to process this crime scene myself.

CHAPTER FIFTEEN

It really *isn't* like it is on TV. That much is true. I head up to the attic, even though Mom keeps telling me to forget it and go to bed. I do *not* want to forget it. And I don't want to talk about it. I want to look at the room. Problem is, first of all, real life is messy as hell. Most of us don't have things so organized that you can tell if a single hair is out of place. The attic is always filled with boxes and junk, and *somebody* never puts things back where they belong anyway. The way I live, every day looks like a crime scene. Every room looks like it's been broken into. It's like I'm mugging *myself*. You see my point.

The point of entry, at least, is clear enough. The attic window is still open. The intruder simply climbed the elm outside, jumped over to the roof, and crawled in through the window. I'm poking around, trying not to disturb anything, but it's impossible. I keep tripping over boxes, and it's impossible to tell if anything has been messed with. I'm trying to think like a criminal. What did he want? Why was he here? Was he on his way downstairs to slit our throats in our sleep? If so, why did he seem to be ransacking these boxes? It's hard to focus. I am tired. And I am scared. And I am angry. It makes it hard to concentrate. This is probably why you wouldn't ask a detective to investigate his own attempted murder. It's clear what I need. I need my sidekick. I need Anoop.

It's well after midnight, but I call him anyway. This is what friends are for, right? You can be in the middle of a big fight and it can be past midnight, but if you really need them, you can call. The phone rings and rings and he does not pick up. But I am not worried. I call again. No pickup, but I'm still not worried. We long ago made a pact that no matter what is going on, if one of us calls three times you *have* to pick up. You just have to. You can be taking a bath or be on the toilet or double-cupping the most beautiful boobs in the world—you have to stop and answer the phone if the other one calls three times in a row. I often imagined the situation in which it might happen, but I never imagined that it actually would happen. I call the third time and okay, I do start to get worried after a few rings. But Anoop, that beautiful bastard, picks up. He sounds tired.

"Hello?" he says.

"Hey, what took you so long to pick up?" I ask. "Were you double-cupping some beautiful boobs?"

"Just my own," he says. "Also, it's the middle of the night and I thought you hated me."

"What gave you that idea?"

"You told me that you hated me. Plus, you were avoiding me."

"You were avoiding *me*!"

"Whatever. What's going on? Did you just call to make up?"

"I wish," I say. "Some crazy stuff went down tonight at Langman Manor." I tell him the whole story. I tell him everything that's gone down since we last talked. I catch him up on the stuff with Jacques and how Hairston helped me. I tell him about the break-in, the cops, all of it. He seems a little annoyed that I called

Hairston and not him to help find Jacques's criminal history and address. But he gets over it. Good friend.

"A real crime," he says. "Hot damn."

"I know!"

"Is anything missing?"

"Yes," I say. "Dad's treasure."

"The *Playboys*?" he asks. "Lisa Baker, Playmate of the Year for 1967? She *is* hot, but you'd think the thief could probably get most of his porn online . . ."

"The coins!" I yell.

"The thief absconded with them?" he asks.

"That doesn't make any sense," I say.

"Only because you won't read that SAT prep book I loaned you."

"No, I mean, I know what that word means—it just doesn't make any sense that some random thief would know how valuable they are. Or even where the coins were situated."

"'Situated'! Nice! You did read the book!"

"I skimmed it," I say. There is a pause. "So what do we do now?"

"Listen," Anoop says. "I'd come over there right now and analyze the balls out of that crime scene, but my parents would kill me. It's late. Tomorrow I'll be at your place at quarter of."

"Quarter of what?"

"Quarter of eight in the morning," he says.

"There's an eight in the *morning*?"

"Be there or be dead," he says.

"Right on," I say. "Right on."

"Rules for Living": The Francis Langman Story
CHAPTER SIX

"Love is not complicated. Women will make you crazy, yes, but love is not any more complicated than a thunderstorm. All you can do is run for cover or face the storm. I always face the storm."

—Francis Langman

Francis Langman married Tammy Reynolds of Bayonne, NJ, the woman who would be his last wife, in 1990. She was a prom queen or something, but also was into metal. She, of course, became Tammy Langman after hooking up with old Fran. They moved to Berry Ridge, NJ, and a son was born. He was given the name of Guy to honor Fran's father. They should have named him Wolf. That would have been so cool. But he was named Guy, and he's tried to do the best with the hand he was dealt. "All any of us can do is try to do the best with the hand we're dealt," Fran would always say. Pretty wise. Still a stupid name, though.

CHAPTER SIXTEEN

The doorbell sings an annoying song, bright and early. I roll out of bed, grab some clothes off the floor, and stumble to the door to let Anoop in. Only it's not *just* Anoop. TK is there too for some unfathomable reason. He looks tired. His jumpsuit is rumpled, and even though he's wearing a baseball hat, his bed head is apparent. He has a Styrofoam cup in each hand, sipping alternately from the left and then the right. He barely looks up to say hello to me as I open the door and invite them in.

"What the hell is he doing here?" I mutter out of the side of my mouth.

"I can hear you," TK says. He takes a sip.

"Well, at least you were considerate enough to get me a coffee." I reach over to take one of the foam cups. TK narrows his already narrow eyes and violently points his elbows up at me to protect the coffee cups. It is a move that reminds me of a documentary I had seen about prison life late one night—it is like I am a fellow con trying to steal his lunch at San Quentin.

"This is not for you," he says in a quiet but firm voice.

"What the hell?" I say. "You got one for Anoop and yourself but not for me? Thanks a lot, TK."

Anoop laughs a pissy laugh and says, "Guess again, Guy."

"What?" I say.

"That second coffee is not for me either," Anoop says.

"You got two coffees for yourself, TK? What the hell? Why are you always so tired? Yeah, and don't tell me research."

"It *is* research," TK says. "And this isn't a second coffee." He holds up the cup in his left hand. "It's tea."

I furrow my brow. He doesn't look at me, so I narrate: "Guy furrows his brow."

TK continues. "It's research to test the effectiveness of various caffeine delivery systems. I've tried coffee. I've tried tea. Now I'm trying an admixture based on alternating sips between the two. I'm trying to figure out the ideal formula to deliver maximum alertness."

"And what do your findings indicate thus far?" I say.

"I'm getting some interesting results," he says. "But there is one problem with this type of research."

"Oh yeah?" I say. "What is that?"

He holds up both cups. "No hands free for taking notes."

"You need a research assistant," I say. "Maybe MF is looking for a job."

"I don't think she'd be interested," he says.

"Me neither," I say. "No offense."

"None taken."

This is the longest conversation I've ever had with TK. He seems all right if a little—okay, a lot—weird. *We're all weird, some of us just hide it better than others. Those who hide it the best are very often the weirdest.*

"So what's the plan, then?" I ask. "Figure out some super-mix of coffee-and-tea hybrid you can bottle and sell for millions?"

He shrugs. "I'm not into it for the money. I'm just in it for the research."

"Okay, listen, you nerds," Anoop says, which is hilarious. "We have some work to do here."

"I'm up, aren't I? And seriously: what is TK doing here?"

"We could use some help."

"Yeah," TK says. "I'm not really sure what kind of help you need. Anoop wouldn't tell me anything. I hope you don't need help moving a fridge or something. I sort of hurt my back."

"I do not want to know how you hurt your back," I say.

"Moving a fridge," he says, narrowing his eyebrows. "What else?"

"Dude, you better give me one of those cups," I say.

"I need them for my—"

"If you say 'research,' I'm going to punch you in your Polish balls."

"Hey," TK says. "What's wrong with being Polish? Copernicus was Polish."

"Copernicus loved the Polish sausage, that's for sure."

"Now we are going to have a problem if you bad-mouth Copernicus."

"TK, you're so weird. Who cares if I talk about Copernicus?"

"Copernicus was a revolutionary genius. The modern heliocentric cosmology *began* with Copernicus."

"Yeah, well, he also was a giant dork who never got laid."

"Who cares if he was?"

"Wow, TK, I don't care if Copernicus got laid. I just feel like breaking your balls. Relax."

"Well, he did get laid. He had a bunch of kids."

"Fine. Copernicus was totally a massive stud who loved to hand out the Polish sausage. Fine."

"Guys," Anoop says. "I hate to break into what is clearly the stupidest conversation I've ever heard in my life and possibly in all of human history, but we have things to do."

"Yeah," TK says. "What *do* we have to do?"

"I was being respectful," Anoop says to me. "I figured I wouldn't tell him anything you didn't want me to tell him."

Great. Now I have to tell TK that my house was broken into. I mean, it's probably public knowledge, but it feels embarrassing. I decide to keep it brief. "Someone broke into my house last night," I say. "The cops didn't do shit. Anoop is going to help me take some prints upstairs. You're welcome to help, I guess."

"Sweet!" TK says. "Real-crime time!" I roll my eyes. Anoop goes for a high five. It's maybe a bit rude, but I leave him hanging.

We head up to the attic. I don't even bother to explain to Mom what we're doing. Could she possibly understand? I highly doubt it. Luckily, she doesn't ask.

"Man," TK says. "It's a mess up here."

"Pardon me for not meeting your standard of housekeeping," I say. "As I said, someone broke in here last night."

"Did they ransack the crap out of the place?"

"Not really," I say. "It was always kind of a mess up here."

"So, what was stolen?" TK asks. "Anything?"

I typically make a habit of not telling anyone that we have thousands of dollars of sunken treasure in the attic, but it doesn't seem to matter much since it's gone now anyway. "Some coins," I say. "Some very valuable Spanish coins my dad found when he was deep-sea diving a long time ago."

"Sunken treasure," Anoop says.

"Whoa," TK says.

"Yeah," I say. "And the thing is—hardly anyone knew he had them. He never talked about it outside the family."

"It seems like the thief knew just what he was looking for," TK says. "There are plenty of valuables up here untouched."

"I guess so," I say, looking around the room. There are various items from Dad's life—small statues, the birth spoon, antiques, and even some jewelry. "None of this stuff is worth anything near what those coins are worth."

"Exactly," TK says. "But none of that would be inherently apparent to your typical middle-of-the-night cat burglar. He wouldn't know those coins are valuable but this other crap isn't."

"Inherently," I say. "Did Anoop loan you that SAT book too?" TK just wrinkles his eyebrows at me.

"Where do we start?" Anoop says. "I'm not sure we can get prints off any of this stuff." He waves his hand at the wreck of the room.

"Do the window," TK says. "That's how he entered, right?"

"Yeah," I say.

"I wish you would have told me what we were doing, Anoop," TK says. "I would have brought some rubber gloves." Anoop smiles, waggles his eyebrows, and pulls a rubber glove out of his pocket.

"That will never not be weird," I say. He laughs. TK snaps the glove on and walks over to the window. He opens it with his gloved hand and steps outside, onto the roof.

"I imagine he climbed that tree," he says, pointing down. "Don't you have an alarm?"

"We have one, but we never use it," I say. I feel like he's going to chide me for that, but he doesn't. He just leaps over to the tree. It's a pretty impressive move.

"So I'm the intruder," he says. "I just climbed this tree. I jump to here—" He hops over to the roof. "And I land like this." His hand almost presses into the wall of the attic, but he stops himself. "Especially in the dark," he says, "it would be almost impossible *not* to touch the wall right about here. I think that will be an easier place to fingerprint than the window itself. That's probably been touched lots of times."

"Just like Anoop's mother," I say, sticking my head out the window. TK rolls his eyes. "Sorry," I say. "Force of habit. But seriously. Great work. That's really awesome."

"So we just need to get some fingerprint supplies and print right around this area," he says, circling his finger in the air. Anoop does that thing with his eyebrows again.

"You did not know why Guy needed help," he says. "But I did." He reaches into his bag and takes out a small box. "Fingerprinting kit," he says. "Top-notch."

"When did you get this?" I ask. It's a really impressive kit.

"I asked for it for my birthday back when we first started talking about fingerprinting."

"You had a birthday?" I say.

"I have one most every year, Guy."

"I had no idea."

"This is why you are a bad friend," he says.

He opens up the small white kit and extracts a small white brush and a clear jar with black powder. "Ack!" he says. "I feel nervous. This is so exciting."

"Are you really nervous?" TK asks. "I guess I could—"

"No," I say. "I'll do it." They both turn their heads at the same exact surprised angle. "What?" I say. "I've done this before. With Zant. An old photo I wanted some information on. I'm a pro."

Anoop hands me the kit. Of course I talk a good game. Can I really lift a fingerprint in this situation? Life is much messier than lab. It's a little windy out there on the roof, and the early-morning sun is making me squint. Part of me wants to let TK do it, or talk Anoop into not being nervous. What if I mess it up? I know you can ruin a scene by messing up a print. There are no second chances.

"Don't forget to glove up," Anoop says. So yet again I am finding myself putting on a rubber glove. My life has gotten weird. I take out the brush and dip it into the powder, just like Mr. Zant showed me back in class. Just the tiniest amount. Delicate movements. Total concentration. A gust of wind rattles the leaves. I wait for it to die down and gently but quickly brush the dust onto the spot where TK estimated the thief would have put his hand. My first attempt brings up nothing but smudges. But my second try shows a clear print. "Quick!" I say. "Hand me the fingerprinting tape!" Anoop rushes to give me a piece of tape and I press it onto the print. I'm so excited that I almost do it too hard, but I calm down and lift the print with the required finesse. I hold it up to the sky and admire my work. Perfect.

"Fantastic!" TK says.

"Really great work," Anoop says.

"Now just one small problem," I say. "What the hell do we do with this?" I climb back into the attic and hand Anoop the print for safekeeping.

"It's true that we can't do too much with it without an exemplar," TK says. I feel happy that I know what "exemplar" means. But bummed because I know he's right. We can't prove anything with just a fingerprint. It's so messed up.

"I'm going to take some pictures anyway," TK says. "It is a

pretty unique pattern. Some double-loop whorls you don't see every day."

"Oh, I see double-loop whorls every day," I say. He takes his phone out of his pocket and takes some close-ups of the print.

"I was looking forward to the Forensics Squad final project," Anoop says. "Kinda disappointing to go from doing it for real back to just pretending."

"Yeah," TK says to me. "That's just what I was telling Anoop's mother."

PART TWO

CHAPTER SEVENTEEN

The day of the Forensics Squad final is here. The Berry Ridge Police have made no progress finding our missing coins, or the thief who took them. Mom has given up, resigned to never seeing them again.

"One of you has to hide in the back," Anoop says. "I'm not getting arrested on the way to a fake crime scene. Too early in the morning for irony."

Anoop and I are almost always alone, so sometimes I forget about the annoying New Jersey law that says you can only have one friend in your car until you turn eighteen.

"Isn't there a religious exception?" I say. "If we get pulled over, just say we're going to church."

"You're Jewish, I'm Hindi, and TK believes in whatever the hell TK believes in," Anoop says. "I doubt the cops will buy it."

"I believe in the Flying Spaghetti Monster," TK says. "I'm a Pastafarian."

"Of course you are," I say.

"Plus, it's Saturday," Anoop says. "The church argument is not gonna work."

"Synagogue?"

"Shut the hell up and get on the floor, Langman," TK says. "I call shotgun."

I crawl in the back and slump down low. It's really

uncomfortable, even with the pillows. Stupid New Jersey. Thankfully, it's a short ride to the golf course.

Anoop parks and we walk toward the clubhouse to find the rest of our crew. The weather is warm, and there are lots of early-morning old guys out, smacking balls around. There are some weird outfits, and I am reminded how Dad always said that he hated golf. "If I want to go smack balls around with a bunch of dudes, I'll go to a boxing match at a nudist gay bar," he'd say. The ball jokes are really easy with golf; it is almost like they are asking for it.

"Hey, look," I say to Anoop, pointing to a sign nearby. "Ball-washing machine."

"My balls are clean," he says. "Seeing as how I visited your mother last night."

"And hey, look at this one," I say. "One-stroke penalty for improper decorum."

"Like having dirty balls?" he says.

"Yeah. Dirty balls. Hey, TK," I say. "Your new nickname is One-Stroke Penalty."

"That doesn't even make sense," he says.

I'm a little punchy from lack of sleep. A little confused (in a good way) that TK is part of the gang. And yes, a little hungry from having missed breakfast. It's sort of combining to make me a little, or maybe a lot, crazy.

"Dirty balls," TK laughs. It's fun to have him on board. We see Mr. Zant and the rest of the group milling about.

"I bet Mr. Zant has dirty balls," I whisper to Anoop. Unfortunately, I've never been terribly proficient at whispering, so Raquel hears me.

"I do not even want to know what *that* means," she says, sliding up to Anoop. I try to explain by pointing to the ball-washing machine, but she rolls her eyes and puts her hand up in my direction and continues ignoring me. Maureen, standing off to the side, smiles just a bit.

Mr. Zant shakes his head with a smile, then clears his throat in a wet, disgusting way. He jumps up on a bench and makes an announcement. "Okay, okay, let's listen up here," he says. It's a bright, sunny morning, and he shields his eyes from the sun while addressing us. I make a show of folding my hands onto my lap and give him an over-the-top wide-eyed smile. He looks pissed, but I know deep down he is amused. Right?

"I have a surprise for you," he says with a sly grin. "I hope you brought your A game."

"Crap," I mutter. "I brought my B through E games, sure, but the A is still at home, on the shelf next to the toilet!"

Zant hears me. "Please don't embarrass me today, Guy," he says.

"*Moi?*" I ask. Speaking French is almost always sarcastic. It makes me wonder how they get anything done in France. People are always just like "*Moi?*" and "*Excusez-moi,*" and no one ever means what they say. How full of it can you get, honestly? But maybe it's different in France. Maybe they say "Excuse me" in pretentious American accents when they feel like being obnoxious?

"Yes, you," he says. "This is not just our final project for the year. This is a contest. Surprise!"

"Ooo-la-la," I say, continuing with the fake French.

"We compete against each other?" TK asks.

"Oh, it's on like Donkey Kong," I say.

"Not quite," Mr. Zant says. "This is a competition, but you will not be competing against each other."

"*Excusez-moi?*" I say.

"Please, Guy, shut up."

"*Le pamplemousse?*" I say.

"Grapefruit?" he asks.

"Yeah, I'm sorry. That's the only other French I know."

"Why are you speaking French, exactly?"

"It's a long story," I say. "But trust me, it makes perfect sense in here." I point to my skull.

"Glad to know it makes sense somewhere," he says. "Because out here?" He draws a circle in the air, with his finger encapsulating basically the entire world. "It doesn't make any sense."

A shrill voice breaks through the morning air. "Ahhh! What is the competition?" Apparently TK isn't the only one excited about competing. I had forgotten how competitive Anoop can be. He is the one yelling, unable to contain himself at the possibility of the game that seems to be afoot.

"Thank you, Anoop," Mr. Zant says, "for getting me back on track. Here's how it is going to work. You five will be a team. An old friend of mine has been running a Forensics Squad from another high school. You will be competing against the Forensics Squad from North Berry Ridge."

"North Berry Ridge?" is the collective shocked cry from our crew.

Mr. Zant waves to a group of students standing across the parking lot. They jog over in unison—yes, actually *jog*, like army recruits in boot camp. They are all wearing the official North Berry Ridge school color—an obnoxious bright orange that permanently damages your eyes just to look at it.

"Stupid North Berry Ridge," I say.

"We got this," TK says to me in a whisper. "Did any of these North Berry Ridge jerkholes actually lift a print from a real crime scene? I think not."

"Plus, just look at them," I say. "They look like a bunch of A-holes with very, very dirty balls." TK laughs. Mr. Zant gives me his "if looks could kill" look. But really, they do look like a bunch of A-holes. Dirty balls being a distinct possibility.

There are five students: a tall Chinese kid, a ragged white kid who has white-boy dreadlocks, a nerdy little dude, and two girls. One of them is a tanned and perfect North Berry Ridge girl and the other is wearing the weirdest outfit I've ever seen. It is a dress made out of crime scene tape. Literally. Like she took a bunch of that yellow DO NOT ENTER tape and sewed it or whatever into a dress. As they approach, they are all whispering to each other and we are all whispering to each other. We all are pretending that we aren't talking about them, but it is clearly what we are doing. Sometimes you have to love the blatant hypocrisy of the human animal. And no, that's not a Dad line—I made that up myself!

"Looks like she doesn't want anyone to enter," Anoop whispers to me. "And I'm guessing a multitude of applicants trying to enter is not a problem she suffers from." Zing!

"She's pretty cute," I say. What? She is. "Good line, though, Anoop," I add.

"Dressed like that? How can you even tell if she's cute? I like that one."

He points to the stunningly beautiful North Berry Ridge Forensics Squad member. Looking at the pretty girl, in addition to the one in the crazy outfit, the Asian kid, the weird one, and the curly-haired kid, I have a strange thought.

"Does anything about their group remind you of anything?" I whisper to Anoop.

"I don't see what you mean."

"They look just like us!"

"That kid's Chinese! I'm Indian."

"Dude, I know, settle down, I'm just saying—"

"That little Jew does look a lot like you, though."

"He does not!" The little North Berry Ridge kid? With that schnozz? And that goofy fro? The guy looks nothing like me! Okay, fine.

"Yeah, he does," Anoop says. "You people all look the same."

"Who even said he's Jewish?"

Smug chin.

"Listen up, everyone!" Mr. Zant says loudly, clearing his throat again to get everyone's attention. "This is my old friend Laura. I'm sorry—Miss Fowler."

Laura, I'm sorry, Miss Fowler, is really pretty. She has caramel-colored skin, a huge smile, and something like a radiant glow. Also pretty impressive cans.

"Thank you, Eric; I mean, Mr. Zant," she says. "I have been training the North Berry Ridge Forensics Squad all year, just as Mr. Zant has been training you. You will find on this golf course evidence of a crime. You must process it, piece together the clues, and solve the case. Please take some rubber gloves and bags to collect materials from the field. After you have gathered evidence, meet back here. We will have the materials you need to process it."

"What do we get if we win?" the pretty girl from North Berry Ridge asks.

"Oh yes!" Mr. Zant says. "I'm glad you asked! It is Sherlock's Glass!"

He reaches into his bag and pulls out a really dorky trophy topped with a gold magnifying glass that looks homemade. I think the fact that it is homemade is supposed to be part of the charm: the teachers are trying to foster ironic competitive lust after this object, like the two schools would compete over it and scheme about it for years to come. "Damn it! North Berry Ridge got Sherlock's Glass." We'd say it slightly tongue-in-cheek, but eventually develop a sincere love for this ironically awesome prize. It would be a great memory and a tradition that would live on.

"When does the contest start?" Maureen asks.

Mr. Zant looks at his wrist. "I just realized that I'm not wearing a watch," he says. Miss Fowler laughs, even though it isn't funny. I say legitimately funny stuff all the time and pretty girls don't laugh. I'm throwing out gold and getting nothing. He forgets that he's not wearing a watch—and no one even *wears* watches anymore—and everyone laughs. What's up with that? Oh yeah. Mr. Zant is handsome. Shut up. Mr. Zant continues: "It doesn't matter that I'm not wearing a watch, however. Because the contest has already started."

"It has?" the little Jew from North Berry Ridge asks.

"Yes," Miss Fowler says.

"Well then, why are we still standing here?" I ask.

"Good question," Mr. Zant says. "You probably should be searching for clues. Please be careful to catalog all evidence. Remember what we discussed about chain of custody and proper handling of evidence. But besides that, just get to it."

"You mean now?"

"If you're waiting for a starter pistol or something, you're going to be here all day. Just go!"

The North Berry Ridge crew walks in tight formation, with their heads down and pencils scribbling. I don't know what they possibly can be writing, but it makes me nuts that they are already ahead of us.

"Dudes, let's get to it!" I yell. We wander in five directions at once. I think Mr. Zant is going to be pissed about it. I think he's going to be mad at how disorganized and unprofessional we look compared to the polished pros from the north. But he doesn't give a shit. He is too busy chatting with Miss Fowler. He is brushing something out of her hair and laughing. They look like a commercial for herpes medicine.

"Me and you, AC Machine," I say. "As always."

"I like your enthusiasm, Guy," he says.

"In it to win it," I say, giving him a fist bump.

We stalk across the golf course, looking under benches and behind trees for anything that might be a clue. All we find is a bunch of golf balls covered in dirt. "Look at all these dirty balls," I say. "So dirty. That's like a billion-stroke penalty." We see the North Berry Ridge kids in a football-style huddle, with the exception of the guy Anoop claims looks like me. He is wandering off on his own. "Let's go see what they're looking at," I suggest.

"Nah, let's go over here," Anoop says. He gestures toward a line of trees. "It's too obvious over where they are. Zant wouldn't hide something in plain sight. He'd probably stick it in the tree line. Make us work for it."

"Miss Fowler can work it, huh?"

"Hells yeah."

We walk up a slight incline toward a thick stand of trees. Dry leaves and pine needles crack underfoot as we make our way deeper and deeper. Minutes pass. Hours pass. Okay, probably not hours, but I'm getting tired of walking. And we've walked a long way. Anoop, as always, is a few paces ahead of me. His lead grows and grows until I am half shouting to make myself heard.

"I think we're getting off track here," I say. "He wouldn't make us go this far—"

"Don't be lazy," he says.

"I'm not lazy, I just—"

"Aha! Ho-ly sheet," Anoop says. "Zant went all out."

"What do you mean?" I say.

"Look at this!" he shouts. "Get your ass up here! Hurry!" I break into a jog, following Anoop's voice. When I catch up, I find him standing over an unbelievably realistic-looking corpse.

"We have a victim," Anoop whispers. "Dude looks like someone."

"Um, yeah," I say. "Some Guy someone." He does look familiar. Is Mr. Zant trying to be cute by making a corpse that looks like me? Ha-ha. Very funny. It's incredibly disturbing, seeing this dead version of myself. What the hell, Mr. Zant? It is disgusting. I almost throw up in my mouth.

"Dude!" I say. "He did go all out."

"Okay, be quiet."

"*You* were yelling!"

"Well yeah, but that was dumb," Anoop whispers. "We don't want the North Berry Ridge jerks catching up. We have clearly discovered the victim. Most important part of the investigation. Everything stems from here."

"It kinda smells like crap," I say.

"It's you," Anoop says. "You smell like crap."

"Shut up."

"So let's begin by determining cause of death."

"I think it probably has something to do with that." I point to the electrical tower looming over us, a few dozen feet away.

"Don't be quick to judge. That could be a coincidence. He could have been bludgeoned, then placed here to throw us off the path." This is pretty far away. He paces it off. "Almost ten yards." He writes this down. "And it doesn't seem like all that much blood, really."

"There's enough to skeeve me all the way out," I say. "Where do you get such a realistic corpse? And this fake blood?"

"Probably Miss Fowler paid for it. She has all that North Berry Ridge money."

"Stupid North Berry Ridge," I say.

"Glove up," he says.

"That's what she said. Aw yeah, give me five, AC. Do it."

Anoop shakes his head at me. "Come on. Take this serious. We can beat those North Berry Ridge jerks."

I put on my rubber gloves even though I am really not enjoying the weird feeling it gives my hands. Anoop snaps his on with too much glee, like a sadistic proctologist about to go to town.

"I'd say from the lack of decomp he's been here not long at all," Anoop says. "No wallet in the back pocket."

"Check the front," I say. "If he had parents like mine, he was always afraid of pickpockets."

"Dude," Anoop says, reaching into the front pocket. "I think you're taking this too seriously. Fake dead bodies do not have parents."

But sure enough, Anoop reaches over and finds a wallet in a front pocket. "Nice work, Detective," he says. "But it's empty. Curious."

It really is impressive. All of it. This corpse is worthy of a Hollywood set. He bags the wallet like a pro, like putting evidence into Baggies is something he's been doing his whole life. He puts a note into his leather-bound notebook.

"I'll check to see if there's any ID," I say. "Maybe in a front pocket." I roll the body over. And that's when I really see the face. It looks like me, but it is no mannequin. It's that kid, the North Berry Ridge kid who looks like me. The truth becomes clear in waves. No, the truth becomes clear like a hammer to the forehead. This is no dummy. This is no setup. This is not part of the exercise. This is not Forensics Squad. This is not an impressive fake corpse. This is a real live corpse. I mean a real *dead* corpse. Whatever, it's the "real" part that is important. Also the "corpse" part. I'm freaking out. I'm freaking out. I'm freaking out.

After that there is a lot of screaming. High, girlish screaming. Mine, mostly. At least that's what they tell me. I black out or something. I'm a person who doesn't like to see dead leaves, much less dead dudes who look like me.

Even now I'm not totally sure what I did. I have to piece it together like clues in a gross jigsaw puzzle. Or like a crime scene investigator, investigating the weirdness of my own life. It seems like what happened was this: Yes, I screamed. A lot. Anoop screamed some too. We are both screaming hysterically, yelling "Oh my God!" and "Holy shit!" and "Holy shit holy shit holy shit holy shit-shit." Stuff like that. Real suave. Someone comes running—I'm still not sure who. Probably either TK or Maureen or both. They deduce the situation and called 911 from a cell phone. The teachers are there in a minute, and my mom shortly after.

Police are showing up, and news vans, and Chopper 4 is hovering overhead. Reporters. Everyone texting like mad. I give some really stupid comment to the press. It is more than a bit of a blur. And then Mom wraps me in a blanket for some reason (why do they always wrap you in a blanket?) and gets ready to take me home. But before I get into the van, Anoop walks close to me and whispers into my ear.

"I've still got the wallet," he says with a wink. "Let's process the evidence tonight."

CHAPTER EIGHTEEN

I go home and immediately fall asleep. You'd think it might be hard to snooze, given the circumstances, but being me, one of the world's greatest nappers, it's not so rough. I sleep. Sleep I can do. Give me a gold star for sleeping. But it is not restful. No, it is not. I dream of maggots. Buzzing maggots. They are the mouths of barking dogs. They are the sky opening with helicopters. They are reporters yelling with tiny notepads. They are me saying stupid things. I don't need Dr. Waters to analyze this stuff. Anyone could analyze dreams, really. They're basically about death or doing it. Man, I should be a shrink. You had a dream about bears? Dr. Langman says: Bears symbolize doing it. You had a dream about soda fountains? Dr. Langman says: Well, that symbolizes doing it. You had a dream about maggots? Well, Dr. Langman says that symbolizes death, unless you're really sort of messed up in the head and maybe you want to do it with maggots. Either way: One hundred dollars an hour, please.

Even the smell of death works into my subconscious. I feel queasy, like the room is spinning. And smelling very bad. I had only ever seen death in the scrubbed-clean funeral home–synagogue–cemetery. And even there I was not cool with it. What is up with the people who talk about death like it is cool? Seriously, death sucks.

When the cell phone does its little insect buzz on my dresser,

I jump. Everything seems scary. Death is everywhere. How did I miss that in my years on this planet? Life ends. This, in fact, is the point of life.

The phone call is from Anoop. He is not feeling so philosophical.

"I called like eight times, you turd sandwich," he says. "You violated our sacred three-call rule. I thought you were dead."

"Nice. I guess that explains the buzzing in my dream," I say. "I was wondering why maggots would buzz."

"You were dreaming of maggots?"

"Yeah. I'm pretty shaken—"

"I'd hate to tell you what I dream about."

"I think I can guess," I say.

"So okay, Langman, I got the wallet. We have some more prints to lift. Let's get on this bitch."

"I don't know, Anoop. It's not a game. That kid is dead."

"Toby," Anoop says. "The kid's name is Toby Weingarten. Was Toby Weingarten. Whatever. It was on the news. Toby was his name-O."

"Okay, so Toby Weingarten is dead. Maybe an accident. Maybe someone killed him."

"Exactly! And we have to catch him."

"No, the *police* have to catch him, Anoop."

"They won't count the wallet if we turn it over. They'll exclude it or whatever. Chain of custody. It's been at my house. I've touched it. You've touched it. Totally contaminated. This wallet is a slut. Everyone's touched it."

"I think they'll understand, given the circumstances," I say.

"They'll *understand*, yeah, but that doesn't matter. A defense lawyer would eat it up and crap it out. Crap it right out."

"But they're going to accept the forensics work of a couple of high school kids, Anoop?"

He ignores this sensible objection. "I'll bring the fingerprint kit over. You did a hell of a job on the window. I want you to process this wallet. And if you want some help, I happen to know some of the best young forensics minds around."

"You?"

"Well, me and a couple of friends."

"Who?"

"You'll see."

"I don't know, Anoop," I say. "It sounds crazy."

"Look," he says. "We owe it to that dead kid to do what we can do to figure out what happened. If someone did this, we need to stop him before he does it again."

I have a creeping weird thought. Is Anoop thinking the same thing? Toby Weingarten could have been one of us. More to the point: Toby Weingarten could have been *me*.

Anoop continues. "And I know whatever we find won't hold up in court, but if we turn the wallet over, they won't even be able to lift prints. They won't do anything with it because it's been contaminated. But if we lift the prints, we can at least make an anonymous tip to the police. That will help put them in the right direction. You know it's the right thing to do."

Oh my. What would the noble warriors of the dong bracelet tribe do? They would gather in the hut and they would do what's right. Or, in the words of Fran, "It's often easy to tell what the right thing to do is, because it's also the hard thing to do." I don't like that one, because it was usually used to make me do something I didn't feel like doing, but it has the ring of truth to it. Certainly now.

"Anoop Chattopadhyay," I say. "Are you calling an emergency meeting of the Berry Ridge High School Forensics Squad?"

"I already did!" he says. "Everyone is in, but I didn't want to start without you."

"*Everyone?*" I ask.

"Yeah, dude," he says. "TK and Maureen were really psyched about it. And Raquel loves fingerprinting. I don't know why, but she's just really good at it." Duh, that's who he meant. I guess I'm going to have to get used to this.

"Where are we meeting?" I ask.

"Um, I was thinking your house," Anoop says.

"Oh, I see," I say. That would explain why they didn't start without me. I am too weary to fight.

"Send 'em over," I say.

"Everyone is pretty much on their way," he says. "Put some pants on and meet us downstairs. People are going to start showing up in about five minutes."

"How do you know that I don't have pants on?" I ask. "Are you spying on me?"

"I know you always nap with no pants on," he says. "Simple deduction."

"Eat shit, Sherlock," I say. I shake my head and click the phone off. Apparently we *are* going to have a Forensics Squad meeting at my house. Pardon me while I skip for joy.

CHAPTER NINETEEN

By the time I get some pants on my lazy ass and make my way down the stairs, it's almost time for the Forensics Squad members to arrive. I'm rubbing my eyes. It feels like the middle of the longest night on earth. In fact, it is about eight o'clock. Mom is in the great room, playing her piano. She's not half bad at it, even though she pretty much just plays the same few sad songs over and over again. She spends a lot of time playing Chopin's Prelude in E Minor, a horrifyingly depressing little number. It's one of those slow piano tunes where every high note rolls like a tear down the piano's cheek and every low note hits you like a punch in the gut. Even the silences between the notes are somehow horrifyingly dismal. Some song. Now imagine it bouncing around the empty walls of an old house with one less person living in it than should be living in it. No wonder I'm depressed.

And yeah, it's really called "the great room." Dad found that funny every time. He'd pretend to be shocked every single time he walked in. "Wow," he'd say, surveying the place as if for the first time, nodding his head in approval with arms outstretched. "This is a great room. I mean, this is really a *great* room."

"Mom," I say. I am standing at the doorway to the great room, only a few feet away, but she doesn't hear me. She is lost in thought, rocking her head, playing the song even slower than normal, tapping out the melody with her right hand and letting long silences sit in between. "Mom!" I shout.

"Yes, Guy?" she finally says without looking up. "What is it? Are you okay?"

What is it? I think. *Good freaking question. What is it about life that makes it so sad? And why do we pretend that it isn't?* I don't say that. And I don't even think about telling her the answer to the second part of her question. Nor do I tell her that Anoop fancies himself some sort of actual detective or forensics expert or whatever. She, like any sensible person on earth, would have insisted that we turn the wallet over to the police immediately. She would have understood that it was not right for high school students to handle evidence in a murder case.

What I say is, "I guess some people are coming over in a little bit. Anoop invited the Forensics Squad. I guess everyone wants to talk about what happened today, or whatever."

"That's good, dear," she says, finishing the song with a loud, pounding flourish and breaking out of her trance. "It's good to talk about things like this. We can schedule an extra visit with Dr. Waters if you like."

"I think *you* should see Dr. Waters," I say.

"Dr. Waters is an expert in *adolescent* psychology," she says.

"Well, you should talk to *someone*," I say.

"I have you, dear."

"Sure thing, Mom," I say. What else is there to say?

"Want me to get some snacks together?" she says.

"If you think that will help," I say.

"I mean, for your friends."

"Oh yeah. Snacks will be good," I say. *What kind of snacks are best for solving a murder?* "Do we have any donuts?"

"No," she says. The quality of junk food in Langman Manor has seriously declined since Dad died. Mom is skinny and youthful-looking, and determined to stay that way.

"Just nothing too weird," I say. "We eat enough arugula at school."

"I wasn't going to bring out arugula," she says, sighing. "I was your age once. Not that long ago. How about popcorn?"

It's probably organic and low-fat and no-salt, but at least it's popcorn. "Popcorn works," I say.

She gets up from the piano, letting a final minor chord ring in the great room as she heads to the kitchen next door. I sit and listen to the silence until the popping of the kernels makes me think of tiny shotgun blasts. It makes me think of the dead kid in the woods. It makes me think of bullet holes. It makes me think of maggots. I wish I had asked for a less violent food. Something soft, like pudding. Crap, I really am an old man. What am I doing with my life?

While she waits for the corn to finish popping, I sit down at the piano bench. Mom was always trying to get me to take lessons, but I never did. I only know one little thing on the piano, that famous four-note riff from Beethoven's Fifth. *Da-da-da daaaaaah. Da-da-da daaaaaah.* I just keep playing that over and over again. Ominous. One thing I'm good at is playing loud, so I don't hear the doorbell ring. I don't hear anyone walk in. But those things must have happened, for when I look up, there is Maureen.

I jump a little bit. *Sheesh.* Why do I startle so easily?

"Sorry to scare you," she says.

"You didn't scare me."

"Okay, good. You don't need any more stress today."

"You got that right," I say. She is being really nice. Are we going to talk more about the events of the day? The thought doesn't make me feel better. Just weird. Maureen senses it, I guess, and changes the topic.

"I didn't know you played the piano," she says.

"I don't," I say. "Just those four notes, really."

"Good enough for Beethoven," she says.

"That's always been my motto," I say.

There is a pause.

"Beethoven had good fashion. He wore some mighty fine ascots, didn't he?" she says.

"You know, I think he did."

Then we just stand there in the great room for a while.

"This is a pretty great room, isn't it?" I say. She does not laugh. Unfortunately, it doesn't sound funny if you don't know that it is called "the great room." And having to explain it doesn't seem worth it. Why do I always say stupid nonsense?

She shrugs and put her hands into the pockets of her hoodie. "It's okay, I guess." Cue awkward pause. *Just keep talking, Gisborne.*

"What did you do with the rest of your surprise day off?" I ask.

"Took a walk, mostly," she says. "I was just walking around when TK texted me about this little meeting or whatever. I was almost here, so I just kept walking."

"Oh yeah, I was going to ask if your mom dropped you off or whatever."

At the mention of the words "your mom," she cringes like the words hurt her ears. She changes the subject fast. "I also wrote some stuff," she says. "I have this online thing. It's no big deal. Totally dumb."

"Sounds neat," I say. *Sounds neat?* What kind of idiot am I? She makes a weird face. She isn't used to compliments, maybe. Or maybe just not from me. She knows it's a good thing, a compliment, but given its source, she remains skeptical. It's like getting a candy bar from your weird neighbor on Halloween, and despite the creamy and tasty exterior you can't help but think that a razor blade is hidden within. Maybe it is. What's wrong with me?

Before that particular question gets answered—for today, anyway—the rest of the Forensics Squad arrives. Anoop comes in first, clomping about in his old-man shoes. He hasn't felt the need to knock at Langman Manor in years. Right behind him comes TK, and then Raquel. I see them make their way up the driveway and wave them in. It is pretty weird that they are at my house. Even weirder is the reason they are there. My mom is popping popcorn and pouring sodas in the other room while we examine the physical evidence of a murder. Just another day in the Langman life.

"Hey, guys, I'll let you be," Mom says, delivering the tray of snacks and drinks. "Just don't get any popcorn on the piano." *Why would we eat popcorn on the piano?*

"Thanks, Mrs. Langman," Raquel says. *Raquel says. To my mom. So weird!*

Mom goes upstairs into a room sadly less great. She is good at making herself disappear—a trait all parents should master. For example, Anoop's dad is always just hanging around, adjusting his toupee, stroking his mustache, and bumping into us when we have things to talk about. Girls, mostly. Maybe he knows that. Maybe he thinks I am a bad influence. Maybe he thinks I am distracting Anoop from the good and righteous path with all my blather. Maybe it's true. Maybe I am doing that. Somebody has to.

I have no idea how this is going to work without Zant. But Anoop does. He takes over like he always does. I should have guessed. He's a leader. Some people are just leaders. Some people are leaders and some people are followers and some people wear ascots and play four notes on the piano. Anoop starts talking in hushed tones.

"Okay, you know why I've called you all here," he says. He pulls the wallet out of a duffel bag. It is still in the plastic evidence Baggie. Totally unmolested. "This was found on the body earlier."

"Hey, what do you mean, 'This was found'?" I say back. "I found it."

"Okay, fine, credit where credit is due. It was Guy who found it. But I found the body."

"That's not really important," Raquel says.

"It's kind of important. For chain of custody," TK says.

"That's exactly right," Anoop says. "I was going to get to that. Chain of custody is what it's all about. It's why we have to do this ourselves. If we turn the wallet in, they won't be able to use it. Even though I've been *extremely* careful, technically it's been contaminated. The best thing for us to do is process it ourselves and anonymously report our findings. It's really the best thing."

"Exactly," TK says. He has a way of saying things with a heavy period at the end that makes you know that arguing would be ludicrous.

"First thing to do would be to lift prints, I guess," Raquel says. *Duh.*

"I think the first thing to do would be to look for any other trace evidence," Maureen says. "Are we sure there's nothing hidden inside? No hairs, even? A scrap of paper? Anything like that could be useful."

"I looked," Anoop says. "There is nothing. Not a penny. Not a single hair. And I had gloves on the whole time, so you won't find my prints."

"I don't know what good prints will even do us," Raquel says. "We know the identity of the kid. It's probably just *his* prints. If he was robbed, the killer wouldn't have dragged the body, emptied out his wallet, and put it back in his pocket, right? If you want to steal a wallet, you just take the wallet. Take the stuff and dump it later. The killer wouldn't have touched the wallet. He didn't want his money. He just wanted him dead."

"Kinda creepy how good you are at that," I say.

"If you want to catch a killer, you have to think like a killer," she says.

"Killer," I say.

TK jumps in. "There are a lot of inconsistencies in the way this went down," he says, pacing around the room. Everyone's still whispering, and it gives the conversation a heated edge. "The body was pretty much in plain view. It was near the electrical tower, but I think too far for it to be suicide." He takes out his camera and flips through some pictures. "I didn't have time to upload these and take measurements, but it just looks a bit too far for a jump. Someone bludgeoned this kid to death, then dragged the body close—but not too close—to the tower," TK says.

"Or they bludgeoned him, *then* threw him off the tower," Raquel adds. She knows a lot about killing people. Seriously: it's kinda creepy.

"Ten yards or so," Anoop says. "I didn't get a chance to measure either, but I think TK is right. Too far to jump."

"I don't know about that," Maureen says. "I mean, it's clear something messed up happened, but I'm not sure we can make any conclusions without—"

Just then Mom sticks her head back in. She is holding a tray with more drinks. Everyone nearly jumps out of their skin. "Mom! Where did you come from?" She says nothing, just gives me the narrow-eyed look. "Uh, that's cool," I say. *What?* I try to shield her view of Anoop with my body. How do I explain this? It feels crazy embarrassing, her catching us playing detective. It feels like I had porn on my screen or something. So cool, Langman, having your mom bring drinks and popcorn into the room filled with your friends. It seems like something a mom should do for you when you're little, not old enough to drive. But no one seems to mind. Cool it, Gisborne, I tell myself. Don't think about it too much. We all have moms, after all.

"I don't know what that is," she says, pointing to Anoop's box of supplies after setting down the tray. "But don't get that on my white rug or I'll kick your ass," she says. Everyone laughs, and with that she leaves.

"Come on, master," Anoop says to me. TK doesn't react, but the girls look pretty surprised. I don't feel like sharing the fact that

I had already proven myself adept at fingerprinting just this morning, so I act like it's normal.

"Don't you know that I'm the fingerprinting master?" I say to the group. "I'm, like, a master. At fingerprinting." Smooth. I put on *another* rubber glove. The now-standard proctology jokes are made and appreciated. I set the wallet on the piano, using it as a makeshift forensics lab. It's much easier in here than in the wind on a ledge. It's feeling familiar, the black fingerprinting powder on the brush. I cover a few spots on the wallet where fingers are likely to touch. The room is silent and airless, like a tomb. "There it is," I say. I don't look too closely at it. I don't want to. I hand it to Anoop. He looks it over. So does TK.

"Um, I think we're going to have to meet in the other room," TK says.

"Dude, not cool," Maureen says to me.

"Don't call me dude," I say. We head into the kitchen. TK squeezes next to Anoop. Anoop holds the print up to the light. They stare at it. "Dude," Anoop says.

"Dude," TK says.

"Dude," I say. "Wait—why are we saying 'dude'?"

"These are some very unusual double-loop whorls," TK says.

"Yeah?" says Anoop.

"Yeah," TK says. "Very unusual, yet I feel like maybe I've seen them before."

"Don't say it," I say.

"Without a doubt," TK says. He brings up another picture on his phone and compares it to the print. "We saw this print before." He shows me the evidence. It's undeniable.

There are lots of confused looks.

"Can I tell them?" Anoop asks.

"Fine," I say, sighing. I feel my face flush crimson.

"This print," he says, almost stuttering. "The same. Here, in Guy's attic. And there, on the dead kid's wallet."

"Wait, what? Is there something you're not telling us?" Maureen asks from the great room. "We can totally hear you. You suck at whispering!" The sound of her voice makes me jump. *Da-da-da-daaaaaah.* Yes, there is . . .

CHAPTER TWENTY

We try to catch the rest of the crew up on what we know. Unfortunately, we have more questions than answers. Who? What? When? WTF? Stuff like that. Before long, it's rather late. Forensics Squad disperses like a bad party. Then it is just me and Anoop. Like most of my life. My sad, short life. It's really starting to hit me. My life *is* going to be cut short. That is clear. Because here's what I'm thinking: These aren't coincidences. Someone—namely Jacques Langman—broke into my house and stole my dad's treasure. Then he followed me to the golf course and tried to kill me. When he realized it was the wrong kid, he tried to make it look like a suicide. Or maybe a robbery. I'm a little unclear on the details, but I'm clear on the culprit. Who else would know about the treasure? Who else would want Toby (me) dead? I'm sure Jacques is the culprit. And I'm sure I'm the intended target. (Okay, sort of sure.)

It's starting to hit me. I'm dead. So sad, really. So many things I wanted to do. Grow a beard. Go to Africa. Punch a moose. (What? One gave me a weird look one time.) Take a pottery class. Skinny-dip in the South of France. Or the North of France, for that matter. The Middle of France—who gives a shit? Hell, I'd even skinny-dip right in the South of Jersey, when you get right down to it. The important thing is being nude on the beach. The important thing is not dying.

Before I get too bummed in that direction, I need to figure

something out. Something is still bothering me from before. Maybe two things. Maybe three things. Maybe a million things. Or I just change the topic.

"Things with Raquel, um, progressing well?" I ask.

"Well, they're progressing," he says, waggling his eyebrows. I sort of don't want to know more. Abort, abort! Change topics again!

"So, um, Maureen was talking about how she was writing stuff," I say. "Some online thing. You know anything about that? Facebook or something?" I ask.

"She probably has a JerseyGoths account. That's what all the local Goth chicks have."

"How would you know that?"

"I know lots of things," he says.

"Have I told you today that I hate you?" I ask.

"I can bring up her account in like two seconds, probably." He whips out his phone and clicks some buttons to go online. "That looks like her," he says. I crowd next to him to see the phone. The name is Neeruam, which seems to be Maureen backwards. Clever.

"Damn!" I say. "How did you do that?"

"You can search by school. She's the only one at Berry Ridge High on here. That chick from North Berry Ridge Forensics is on here too. You can send her a message, since you love her or whatever."

"I do not love her."

"What do you want with Maureen's page? Want to read her entry from today? I think it's about her mom."

I read some of her writing about her mom and I think I have a new understanding of Neeruam. Maureen. Whatever. How weird it must be to grow up with a MILF-y supermodel for a mom. You probably always feel like you can't keep up. So you try to be perfect in school. You try to find your own thing—maybe you dress in a way guaranteed to piss your mom off. People are so predictable; they just never see it about themselves.

Shit. Who am I to talk? Maybe this is my life. Maybe a kid of a man who did everything would try to be someone known for doing nothing. Maybe I'm who I am because I realize I can never be my father. Maybe this is why we all are who we are.

"Are you okay?" Anoop asks. "Why is it taking you so long to read?"

"Just thinking," I say.

"Thinking about how effed up this is?" he asks. "About how we're going to catch this killer?"

"Something like that," I say.

"There's more," he says. "Here is yesterday's. It looks like poetry."

"Wait," I say. "So you're telling me that Maureen writes in a secret journal with black ink on black pages so no one can read it, but then posts it online for the world to read?"

"It would seem that way," Anoop says. "Girls are pretty freaking weird."

"Sure are," I say. "So yeah, open that entry."

"Neeruam wrote a poem about forensics," he says. "Ha-ha."

"Really?"

"Really."

"She really wrote a poem about forensics? Probably about the handsome Mr. Tnaz."

"What?" he says.

"It's Zant backwards," I explain.

■ 157 ■

"Got that," he says. "But did you just call Zant handsome?"

"Shut up," I say. "Show me the poem, Poona." Saying names backwards is fun.

"It's about fractography."

"Who would write a poem about fractography?"

"I think we both know the answer to that."

"Can I just read it?" I say. He hands me the phone.

> fractography
>
> to understand
> how things break
> you need to
> break things yourself
> and watch what happens
>
> i study how things break
> shattered windows
> busted glass
> a human being
> a heart
> a girl
>
> breaking things is easy
> to study how to break things
> you need to break (them) yourself
>
> putting them back together
> is science

and art
and luck
and sometimes
not possible at all

"Not bad," I say. "Not that I know anything about poetry outside of 'There once was a man from Nantucket.'"

"Greatest poem ever written," Anoop says.

Then I see another poem. It appears to be called "The Guy of My Dreams." This one I read aloud.

the guy of my dreams

the guy of my dreams is an unfinished
    boy:
a question mark, an ellipsis.
a shrug of the shoulders, a roll of the
    eyes
an untied shoe
unkempt hair
and softly whispering heart.
the guy of my dreams is a wounded soul
a wingless bird
a teddy bear in a suit of armor
a silk pillow that hides a knife inside.
and someday,
someday,
that guy becomes a man
and someday,

someday,

that guy takes my hand.

someday.

someday . . .

. . . ?

"Man," Anoop says. "Holy sheet. How did I not see it before? Neeruam likes you."

"Stop calling her that. And she does not."

"The *Guy* of my dreams."

"It just means guy, any guy, not Guy-Guy."

"If you choose to delude yourself, Guy-Guy . . ."

"It's not a delusion."

"That poem is very clearly about you."

"Are you saying I'm a teddy bear in a suit of armor?"

"I would probably say an asshole in a T-shirt, but close enough."

"Thanks."

"So, Guy-Guy," Anoop says. "Listen. I know what you're thinking. The prints on the wallet matching the prints in your attic. The fact that Toby looked like you. It's a little creepy."

"It's a lot creepy!" I say.

"Are you thinking what I'm thinking?" he asks.

"Usually when you ask that, the answer is no, because you're thinking about math and I'm thinking about boobs, but in this case we quite possibly are in agreement."

"Hey, I think about boobs too," he says. "It's like sixty–forty, boobs to math."

"I got about ninety–ten, boobs to video games."

"*Boobs to Video Games: The Guy Langman Story,*" he says. "That should be your autobiography."

"Okay, well, it's going to be a short one. I think someone is trying to kill me."

"And are you thinking you know who it is?"

"Is that what *you're* thinking?" I ask.

"Let's just say the name of the guy who wants to kill you, one, two, three: One, two, three . . ."

"Jacques Langman."

"Jacques Langman."

"He's obviously around," I say. "Seeing as how he came to the funeral."

"And pretty much nobody else knew about the coins."

"And the criminal record, and it's all just . . ."

"Okay, okay," Anoop says. "But let's not jump to crazy conclusions."

"I'm just not sure what other kind of conclusions we could make."

"Listen. It's late. I gotta run. Good night, man. Tomorrow we look for more clues."

"Clues about the impending murder of Guy Langman or clues about Neeruam and the mystery of why girls are so hard to figure out?"

"Both."

"Deal."

"Deal."

I head up to my room. I get out my notebook. I think maybe I should try writing my own poetry. Words of Dad's, old proverbs, thoughts and fears breaking across the page like waves. I'm not much of a poet, though. Not really. I did write a kick-ass haiku about a robot once. My favorite poem really is the one about that guy from Nantucket. It's got everything, if you think about it. Whitman is okay, but he really can't hold a candle. But tonight I don't feel like writing—not poetry, not my book on Dad, not anything. I just stare at a blank page and ask it the same question over and over again until the word doesn't even seem to mean anything, until it is just funny squiggles of black on white: Why? Why? Why? Why? Why? Why? Why?

CHAPTER TWENTY-ONE

I'd love to sleep in, but crime waits for no man. Or something. Anyway, Anoop calls me early the next morning. He's already been working on answering at least one-half of the mysteries on our plate. He's been doing some reading. "They aren't releasing much about the cause of death on Toby. They have determined that the fall is what killed him, though. He wasn't bludgeoned before the fall."

"Unlike the theory of your creepy girlfriend."

"Raquel is not creepy!"

"She is sort of good at figuring out the mind of a murderer, though."

"It's part of the skills of being a good detective. Zant said that all the time."

"Maybe Zant killed Toby. Zant sure knew a lot about the mind of the killer."

"Why would Zant kill Toby?"

"Probably just jealous over how handsome he was. I don't know if you noticed, but Toby was a really, really good-looking fellow."

"You're clearly just saying that because he looked like you," Anoop says. "Which brings us back to our previous theory."

"Whatever, whatever. Sure, sure. So what do we do next?"

"The way I see it is, we do one of two things," Anoop says.

"We either go back to the scene of the crime and look for clues, or we try to find Jacques Langman ourselves."

"Those sound like terrible ideas," I say. Because they do. "Isn't there a third thing?"

"Well, there is, but I already did that this morning."

"Nice."

"So you choose, my friend. What do you think will bear the most fruits, as it were?"

"By 'third thing' I mean call the police, not whatever weird third thing you had in mind," I say.

"The police aren't going to care, Guy," he says, and I know he's right. "We have to do this ourselves."

"Then let's get to the golf course," I say. It's the least frightening of the two options. "At least we aren't going to get killed there."

"Unless you can die from dirty balls."

"Which, if you can, you already would have. Are we allowed to just go walk around the golf course?" I ask.

"I think so," he says. "It's not like you have to pay to get in."

Turns out you totally have to pay to get in.

We drive all the way over there only to get turned away by a snooty turd in a cardigan sweater. He's like some sort of golf-course guard-Nazi in a little booth.

"You boys can't just show up here looking like bums and defile this course," he says. "It's a public course, yeah, but there's a dress code and a fee."

I mutter, "You dick, you have dirty balls," and shuffle off. Anoop has no intention of being dissuaded so easily.

"All we have to do is dress like golfers?" he asks the guy in the booth. The guy nods.

"I think my pink sweaters and lime-green slacks are at the cleaner's," I say.

"I'm sure your dad had some stuff that would pass as golfwear," Anoop says to me. "He probably had some clubs too."

"Dad hated golfing," I say.

"Okay, you can go without clubs. You can be my caddy."

"I ain't your caddy, bitch," I say. "You're my caddy. Who's your caddy?"

"I'm the Bengal Tiger Woods."

"Good one."

We drive back to my house on the slightly absurd mission of finding clothes that will allow us to pass the rigorous standards of the golf-course police. Anoop is right, though. Fran probably had lots of clothes we could use for the purpose. We get to the Manor, park the car, and head into my dad's old office. There are enough rooms in Langman Manor that it isn't exactly like one of those creepy houses where a shrine to a dead person lingers long after they are gone. It is just a room filled with crap we haven't bothered to get rid of. Okay, possibly for shrine-like reasons. Mom likes to go in there and look around at Dad's old stuff. Once I saw her wearing one of his old shirts—a polyester Hawaiian number decorated in scores of ukuleles and topless Polynesian ladies— and talking to herself in the mirror, as if she were him. She looked so happy that I didn't want to interrupt. Funny thing is, she hated that shirt while he was alive.

It doesn't seem like Polynesian tits would be the right motif to go golfing in, much less to appease Mr. Golf-Nazi, who is working the check-in booth, but Anoop insists.

"Dude," he says. "That is the funniest shirt I've ever seen in my life." He takes a few pictures with his phone. I model. Work it.

Stuff like that. Anoop picks out a pretty funny '80s-looking pink shirt and a pair of pink pants. Fran was pretty large for much of his life, his waistline of an epic girth, so we have to cinch up the pants with ginormous belts. It is a pretty weird look.

"Don't we need golf shoes?" I ask.

"I'm pretty sure you're thinking of bowling."

"I'm not thinking of bowling."

"You're thinking of sticking your fingers into some balls, that much I know," he says.

"That doesn't even make sense, Anoop," I say.

"Come on," he says. "Let's roll."

"Now *you're* thinking of bowling," I say.

"I'm thinking we need to get moving."

"Shouldn't we bring some clubs?"

"Small detail," he says.

"Dad did have golf clubs somewhere," I say. "He got them as a gift. Never used them." We look through his office closets, unearthing boxes of papers and pictures of him as a young man, vivid and alive. I get sucked in, staring at the pictures, thinking about his life. The hair on that man! The hats! The ascots!

I find pictures of me too. Baby pictures. Kid pictures. Pictures of me hyper—playing baseball, grinning at the camera under an oversized blue batting helmet even though I don't remember ever actually being happy playing baseball. Or maybe I was. I am happy in all the pictures, hanging on my father's arm, both of us grinning like chimps. I'm smiling in every one of them. It's hard not to think about what this means and how different it is from my life now. I see a bag of golf clubs and pick it up.

Then I find a lined yellow piece of paper. It's folded in half. I open it up. Dad's handwriting. A simple note. To whom? To himself? I read it and my eyes immediately fill with tears.

"What's that?" Anoop asks.

"Nothing," I say. "Nothing at all." I tuck it into the pocket of my absurd pants. "Let's roll."

We drive to the golf course, park among the expensive cars, and haul our golf clubs across the lot. We look ridiculous—me in a Polynesian titty shirt and Anoop all in pink—but no one seems to notice. Is it that our clothes fit in here? Or that they're so distracted whacking their balls? Golfers are an obsessive bunch of weirdos.

We get up to the desk and I'm happy to see that there has been a shift change. The annoying guy who gave us the stink-eye is gone, and in his place is a big fat guy who just seems interested in listening to talk radio and making out with a bag of Funyuns. We walk by in our ludicrous golf clothes and pretend we are going to go golf. As discussed, we figured we'd bust out some golf lingo to seem like serious players in case anyone was listening.

"The wind is looking mellow. I'm totally going to hit a bunch of boogies," I say, just in case the other players think that maybe we were fakers. (Which we of course are.)

"I'm pretty sure it's 'bogeys,' ass crack," Anoop says.

"And I do declare that it's boogies," I reply. When I'm being fancy, like I think a golfer should be, I end up talking in a British accent. Anoop hates this, presumably because of India's colonial history with the British. That's right, I *was* paying attention in Social Studies, Mrs. Lewis!

No one is visibly impressed by my golfery lingo, but I'm pretty sure deep down they appreciate how awesome I am. Either way, it doesn't matter. We aren't actually there to play. We are on a different mission. We are there to look for clues, whatever that means. I figure I'd just whack a ball into the tree line, giving us an excuse to poke around in there. The idea of being at the spot where that body was found creeps me out a bit, but I take a deep breath and go for it. Someday maybe I'll be able to wiggle my finger inside a bullet hole to determine its caliber. Maybe not. But for now at least, I have to be okay with being near where a dead body was. I mean, it's not even there anymore. Quit being creeped out, Langman. Get used to this.

It turns out that it is hard to hit a ball into the tree line (how do you actually hit it into a tiny hole a thousand feet away?), so I just pick one up and throw it in the general direction of where we want to hunt for clues. Golfery stink-eyes are given, but who cares? I'm not really all that good at throwing for distance and accuracy, so this takes a few tries as well. Finally. Sheesh.

"Oh Lord, whatever has happened to my ball, Anoop?" I say.

Anoop resists the ball joke for once and rushes off into the weeds. Or into the rushes! He rushes into the rushes. Because "rushes" are a kind of grass? Never mind. The ball is in the bush. (Ha-ha.) We use our clubs like machetes and enter the thicket, methodically chopping.

There is police tape marking off the scene, but only the small clearing where the body was found. No one is guarding it. No one seems to be looking for the killer. Maybe they don't care who killed him? Or maybe they already know? Is this already a closed case? Do they have a suspect? Jacques Langman? No, couldn't be. No one knows except me.

"What are we looking for, Anoop?" I ask. "I mean, not that

this place is giving me the creeps and not that I'm afraid of birds, but ah! Did you hear that? A coyote?"

"Coyotes rarely swear, do they? That was just one of those dumb-ass golfers shanking, or slicing, or whatever."

"What are you doing?"

"Climbing a tree."

"I can see that, but why? What are we going to find?"

"A clue."

"Such as."

"Look at me, Guy, it's dramatic."

"What?"

"I'm holding a clue." I look up. And indeed he is. It's a shred of fabric. Not just any fabric, but an obnoxious piece of orange fabric.

"North Berry Ridge orange," I say. "What does it mean?"

CHAPTER TWENTY-TWO

After our trip to the golf course, I decide to go home and take a bath. Sometimes I like to go all out, light some candles, use the scented oils. Make a mountain of bubbles. Don't judge me. It's relaxing. Blissful, even. I am just about really slipping into a beautiful bath coma when I am rudely interrupted. The door flies open and bangs the towel rack with a noise like a shot. I jump up, then dive back down into the tub with its obscuring bubbles. Because I have company. It's not just Anoop—who has entered the bathroom on me before—but Maureen Fields and TK!

"Wha-wha-what are you guys doing here?" I say, checking the bubbles to ensure adequate wang coverage. Like I said, I use lots of bubbles, so I am safe. Still. "Please tell me Raquel isn't coming," I say.

"We called your cell like nine times," Anoop says. "You are not taking the three-call thing seriously. So we came over. Your mom let us in. We called R, but she wasn't around."

"Sorry, Guy," I hear Mom yell in a singsong from the hallway. "That Anoop can be quite charming. Let me know if you need a towel."

"I don't need a towel. I need these assholes to leave me alone!"

"That's enough," Mom says.

"Wow," says TK. "You curse in front of your mom?"

"What are you doing here?" I say, choosing not to answer his question, but rather posing a more pressing one of my own.

"You didn't hear?" he asks, in that little drawling way he has of talking. He turns to the others. "Oh, I guess he didn't hear."

"How would I hear anything?" I say.

"Internet?" he says.

"Um, I'm in the bathtub?" I say. I give Maureen a "what the hell?" look. She smiles.

TK gets out his phone and reads: " 'Coroner Adams announced today that Toby Weingarten's death was ruled a suicide. The case is considered closed.' "

"What about the clue we found?" I ask, somewhat agitated.

"Wait, you guys found a clue without us?" Maureen says. She sounds mad.

"Yeah," I say. "You didn't tell her, Anoop?"

"I didn't have time," he says.

"We found a piece of fabric in a tree at the golf course," I say.

"Not just a piece of fabric, but a piece of orange fabric," Anoop says, tapping his temple with his finger. "North Berry Ridge orange." He takes an evidence bag out of his pocket and shows it to Maureen and TK.

"Interesting," TK says.

"Impressive," Maureen says.

"It was quite a piece of undercover detective work," I say. "We had to dress up like golfers and everything."

Maureen laughs. "Oh man, I'm sorry I missed seeing you in your golfer outfits," she says. "Now I'm really mad at you." But she doesn't sound it.

"Ha-ha," I say. And for a second I forget that I'm in a tub. I forget that there are other people in the room. "I just don't believe it about Toby," I say.

"If you look at the comments in the article," TK says, "lots of other people don't either. They say the ruling happened too fast. They say that Adams just does what the mayor tells him. They say that if the mayor wants to cover up a murder, he does it. Murders look bad for the city, and the mayor wants to get reelected, and—"

"I don't want to cut you off," I say, cutting him off because I suddenly remember where I am. "But we're going to have to continue this later. These bubbles aren't going to last forever. This show is about to go from PG-13 to R-rated real quick. Strong chance of NC-17."

"Okay, no problem," Maureen says. "Text me later."

Do I have Maureen's number? No, I do not. She turns to the steamed-up mirror and quickly writes her digits with her finger on the steam. "I have to go anyway. Oh, and sorry I can't do that with my feet," she says.

"Me too?" I say. The guys laugh. TK and Maureen head out. Anoop remains. I don't think he'll be seeing anything he hasn't seen before. Once the door is closed, I get out of the tub.

"What the hell was that?" I say.

"Hurry up and get dressed," he says. "New York is a pretty 'anything goes' kind of city, but I'm pretty sure we'll get kicked off the bus if you're buckass naked."

"Wait, what?" I say. "Did I miss something?"

"Well, I thought the context clues would give you an inkling. Do I have to spell it out for you?"

"Yeah," I say. "Please spell it out for me. I'm not thinking straight at the moment."

"Is it because Neeruam totally gave you her phone number?"

He points to the number written in steam on the bathroom mirror. He wiggles his eyebrows. "I'll put it into my phone for you in case the steam goes away."

That's definitely *not* why I wasn't thinking straight at the moment, but I'm glad that it diverts Anoop's attention for a moment. While he's entering Maureen's digits into his phone, I grab a towel. I wrap myself in its fuzzy warmth and roll my eyes at him. I head down the hall to my room to get dressed. He tries to follow, still peering into his phone, but I'm quick. I slam my bedroom door in his face and quickly lock it.

"I'll just wait out here, then," he says through the door.

"Good idea," I say. "So what the hell are you talking about New York for?"

"There is just one place for this investigation to go," he says. "Or rather, there's one place for us to go. New York, baby."

"What on earth for?" I ask, though I think I already know. My stomach is tightening around the thought. It's like a rock in my gut.

"We can sit around and wait for Jacques Langman to strike again," he says. "Or we can go to him. I say we take the battle to the enemy, disrupt his plans, and confront the worst threats before they emerge."

"Are you quoting the Bush Doctrine?" I ask.

"And you say you weren't paying attention in history class!" he says. "Guy, I'm so proud of you."

"Whatever. It's a stupid doctrine. I don't like any doctrines. Not the Monroe Doctrine. Not the . . . um, that's the only other doctrine I can think of, but the Monroe Doctrine sucks! And so does this one. It's a horrible idea. What are we going to do? Just go knock on his door, and when he opens it we say, 'Hey, here I am, kill me now?'"

"Well, no, we don't do that, in part because he lives in an apartment, so we'd have to press his buzzer and get him to buzz us up. *Then* he kills you." Funny.

The rock in my stomach gets bigger and heavier. I remember that I mentioned to Anoop that I found Jacques's address with Hairston's help. Anoop is not going to let this go. He does *not* believe in letting things go. It's the Anoop Doctrine. I'm mostly dressed, so I open the door.

"This is not funny!" I say. "What if he does try to kill me?"

"Dude, I thought it through," he says. "We don't ring his buzzer, we wait outside. We do some surveillance, wait until he leaves. Then we confront him in a public place. He can't stab you in the face in public. Somebody would be sure to notice."

"Dude," I say. "This is New York we're talking about."

"Okay, yeah, but he can't just kill you on the street. We wait until he's in a big crowd. We ask him what the hell this is about. If he runs, it's as good as admitting his guilt. Plus, I'm packing heat." He taps his pocket. Does he have a gun in there?

"Wait. What?"

"Just kidding. I might bring a kitchen knife, I guess."

"Good. That way we can make him a salad if he tries to kill us. But really, I'm still not sure we can . . . ," I start to say. Then I have a simple revelation.

"What?" Anoop says.

"We don't even have to find him," I say. "We just fingerprint his doorknob! Make a match. Home in time to finish up the bubble bath."

"Dude, you're a genius!" Anoop says. He says it with total conviction. He's one hundred percent sure I'm a genius. Why don't I feel like one?

While I finish drying my hair, Anoop gets out his phone and brings up a map, bus schedules, all that. He starts flicking the screen with dramatic gestures, like a magician.

"Sorry to say it's too late to go tonight, but we can catch an early bus tomorrow."

"Yeah, so sorry that I can't go get murdered as soon as freaking possible."

"You're not getting murdered. Look, that address is in Chelsea. Could someone get murdered in a place named for a girl?"

"Probably, Anoop," I say. "What the hell do I know about Chelsea?"

"It looks easy enough to get to." He hands me the phone. I stare at the dizzying grid of streets that make up New York. I read the labels on the map. It's like an impossible maze, and I'm a hungry rat trying to find the cheese. Except, of course, here the cheese is actually a guy trying to kill me. What the hell am I doing?

"Let's just steer clear of the Meatpacking District, okay?" I say, handing back the phone. "We can get in and get out. So to speak." Anoop laughs. It really does say "Meatpacking District" right there on the map. It also shows a Flatiron District and some-thing called the Museum of Sex. New York is weird.

"Maybe one detour, though, right?" he says.

"Museum of Sex?" I say. "High five!"

"No, dude," he says, taking the phone back. "Eugene Lang

is right there. The college? Didn't you say a while ago that you wanted to go there?"

"Did I? Probably just because it has a funny name. Hello, I go to Eugene Lang. Ha-ha. A college named Eugene. Plus, I'd be a Lang-man. I'm Guy Langman, a Eugene Lang-man. Hilarious. But now I'm leaning toward Slippery Rock."

Anoop sticks out his bottom lip and cocks his head. He puts his hands on his hips. "Really? That's great. I didn't know you had a school picked out. I know it's in Pennsylvania, but what else? Are they strong in the sciences, or . . ."

"Um, I'm not really serious about going there, Anoop," I say. "I just like the name. I'm just kidding around."

"Well, it wouldn't hurt to visit a college while we're in the city," he says. "Maybe it will spark something. Most everyone at school already has their colleges ranked, and some are already applying."

"Most everyone at school has had their colleges picked out since they were in preschool. Maybe since they were in diapers. I'm just not that guy. Let it drop, Anoop, please," I say. "We're going on this trip to try to catch the guy who is trying to kill me. Can we just focus on one thing at a time? If I make it through junior year without getting murdered, maybe then I will worry about colleges."

"You promise?"

"Promise," I say.

"High five," he says. High five. "Okay, dude, this is going to be awesome. We can catch the early bus. It leaves from that limo place near the mall. I'll pick you up bright and early."

"Those are my two least favorite things: brightness and

earliness. And wait, what? The bus? What are we, twelve? Why aren't we driving into the city like men?"

"Possibly because some of us don't know how to drive, like children," he says, none too kindly.

"Okay, yeah, but what about you?"

"My mom will kill me if I take the car into the city. She'll know too because of the E-ZPass. She studies that thing like a hawk."

"Is she afraid you're taking secret late-night trips to the Meat-packing District?"

"Very funny," he says. He's right. I am very funny.

"Also: very manly of you to not be allowed to drive some-where because your mom says. You could totally take down the E-ZPass and pay cash. But no, your mommy says you have to take the bus. Awww."

"Didn't you take the bus to school the other day, Guy?"

"Shut up, Anoop."

"Ha-ha. You rode the bus with Penis-Head."

"Rub it in, jerk."

"That's what your mother said."

"Nice."

"Now get some rest. I really hate driving in the city and, fine, that's why we're taking the bus."

Yes, it seems as though one should always be well rested when meeting a killer. I want to die like I live. Actually, I don't want to die at all.

CHAPTER TWENTY-THREE

The early bus to New York is always crowded. Always tons of people from the Jerz heading into the NYC. They call Berry Ridge a bedroom community, which means that a lot of people who live here actually pretty much just sleep here. They spend the rest of their time working in New York City. Or, presumably, they actually spend most of their time getting to New York City. It's a long ride.

"How long is this going to take?" I ask Anoop, getting bored even though we're barely out of town. "And why do you get the window seat?"

"Well, it is only twenty-six-point-two miles to the Port Authority," he says, checking his phone, ignoring my second question. "So about an hour if we're lucky. But we probably won't be lucky. I'm seeing a lot of traffic."

"Hey," I say. "I never realized that Berry Ridge is twenty-six-point-two miles from the city. Isn't that how long a marathon is? We could just run it."

"Have you been secretly training for a marathon in between naps and video games, Guy?"

"No, but man, it is pretty amazing that it takes us longer by bus to go twenty-six miles than it does for some people to run it."

"Just think if we had a horse."

"Progress is pretty weird," I say.

"Yeah, but it does have its perks," he says, shaking his phone.

"If somehow we could live in a world without traffic, but *with* smartphones," I say.

"Well, let's make the most of our time here," he says. Man, I think, Anoop is deep. We only have so much time in life. Our days are a finite resource. Then I realize that he's not being philosophical, he just means we should use our time on the bus wisely. "We should be talking about plans, anyway," he says. "What are we going to do when we find Jacques? Are we even going to recognize him?"

It takes me a second to snap out of my thoughts, to deal with the pressing issue of finding Jacques and hopefully staying alive in the process. "We'll recognize him," I say. "He looks a lot like my dad, uh, did." That comment sits quietly for a moment.

"I still can't believe Fran is gone," Anoop says. The bus bounces over a pothole. "Sucks."

And this, if you'll pardon me for saying so, is why I love Anoop. When you lose a parent, people don't know what to say. They're afraid of saying the wrong thing. So often they don't say anything at all. Which, weirdly enough, is the wrong thing. Say something. Say anything. Just "Dude, I'm sorry that happened" or one of the canned lines like "I'm so sorry for your loss," even though there is no reason to apologize. Or just say "Sucks." Just say that. Just say one word. "Sucks." It's better than saying nothing. Side note: What's up with saying that you "lost" a parent? He's not a sock. He's not a mitten. He's not a lucky baseball card. I didn't *misplace* him. I know right where he is. The problem is that he's dead.

"Yeah," I mumble. (What, you thought I was going to say that out loud to Anoop about how I love him?) "Sucks."

The bus rumbles along slowly, lurching, then stopping;

lurching, then stopping. Good old Interstate 80. Good old New Jersey Transit. Signs for Clifton, Fair Lawn, Passaic, East Rutherford. "Do you think Fair Lawn has a complex about only being fair?" I ask Anoop. "Wouldn't they rather be Great Lawn? Why don't they let me name towns?"

"Good question, Guy," he says. "And it's very interesting to think about what Fair Lawn thinks about being only a fair lawn, but we need to formulate a plan here. I brought the fingerprinting kit, of course—"

"Of course," I say, like it would be ludicrous to ever leave the house without it.

"Because why force a confrontation if you don't have to, right?" he says. "All we really have to do is get one of his prints and we can compare it to the—"

"Exemplar," I say.

"Exemplar," he says, smiling. "And we can know if he's the one who was on your roof without ever having to confront him. If we go to the police with that, they'll have to do something, right?"

"One would think," I say.

The traffic gets thicker. The bus goes slower. The tunnel is up ahead. For long periods of time we're just sitting, vibrating in the bus. I want to puke. Before long we are descending into the tunnel's mouth, inching along in menacing darkness. Every time I'm in the tunnel, I can't help but think how amazing it is that humans built this. This entire tunnel, big enough and strong enough to withstand millions of cars. Under water. You can't help but think that nerds built this tunnel. What would the world be like without our nerds?

And before too long, the tunnel barfs us back into daylight, into the bustle of the Port Authority. It's hard to believe how many people are going in all directions at once. I'm sort of in awe every time I come here, stopping to stare at the diverse millions— a Hasidic Jew in a Yankees cap, an African woman in a bright orange head wrap and matching flowered dress. A homeless guy peeing in a trash can. Ah, New York.

"Hey, watch it, buddy," a New Yorker says behind me, shoving me out of the way.

Anoop is off and running, not quite literally, but almost. He's moving quickly, on a mission. His long legs are a blur as his thin form darts through the human traffic. "Come on," he says. "This is getting exciting."

"Can't we take a cab?" I say.

"What am I, made of money?" he asks. He does it in an impression of an old Jewish man, and it makes me smile. "It's only a mile to his place. Follow me!" He's off through the doors of the bus station into the street, eyes darting between reading directions on his phone and the street signs. As always, I'm tagging along, trying to keep up.

Anoop strides through the traffic like a pro while I cower on the curb, waiting to make sure every car is going to stop. He's confident that they will. He's confident that the world will treat him well. And it does.

After twenty minutes of brisk walking, we're in the part of the city known as Chelsea. Jacques's address is on Twenty-first Street. It's a nice enough neighborhood. Crowded, but peaceful. The street is lined with trees and there is a nearby park. But it's not like home. The buildings are huge. You get a weird sort of vertigo staring up into the giant buildings. You also get people who push past you, annoyed by the gawking tourist. Everyone in New York seems very annoyed all the time. The horns honk endlessly, like the squawk of irritated birds. Why would you want to live here? Those are my thoughts. Also: We're screwed.

Anoop is standing, staring at the building that must match the address of where Jacques lives. It's an *enormous* high-rise, with what must be hundreds if not thousands of apartments in it. I look at the much-handled doorknob, the people coming and going, and I realize that there is no way we can lift a print off of anything. How in the world are we going to find him?

"I know what you're thinking," Anoop says. "I have to admit that I didn't quite see this coming."

"There must be a million people who live in that building," I say. "This is totally impossible." We're standing there looking at this enormous building and I feel incredibly small. I feel like curling up in a ball on the sidewalk and weeping. Only, you know, the sidewalk is kinda gross.

"Maybe not *totally* impossible," Anoop says. "We just have to get into the lobby. Take this one step at a time. Of course— there is a slight impediment to that first step." He points to the building's doorman, a dude the size of a large refrigerator looming near the entrance. He's wearing a red velvet uniform and has on a hat that should belong to a boat captain or an officer in the Marines.

"Hey, why do doormen wear those stupid hats?" I ask, mainly because I can't think of anything resembling a plan to get past him.

"Those hats aren't stupid, Guy. They are . . . wait for it . . . adorable. Get it? Like a-*door*-able?" Anoop says.

"Yeah, got it," I say. "Hilarious."

"Adorable," he repeats, cracking himself up. He slaps his knee.

"Are you stalling because you have no idea what to do next?" I ask.

"No!" he says. "I'm . . . I'm . . . well, yeah, that's what I'm doing." At least he's being honest. And then I have a brainstorm!

"Got it!" I say. "You run up to him and start cursing in Arabic. He'll think you're a terrorist and chase you down the street. I'll sneak in while he's away from his post."

Anoop doesn't seem to love this idea. He shoots me with eye bullets. "I don't speak Arabic, Guy."

"I know that," I say. "But I bet Captain Doorman doesn't either. Just yell something that sounds Arabic. It's bound to succeed!"

"Succeed at what, getting me arrested?" he asks.

"Hey, you don't hear me complaining," I say. "And I'm probably going to end up getting killed here."

"Um, I *do* hear you complaining, Guy," he says. "It's essentially all I've heard every moment of this trip."

"Pardon me for not wanting to die."

"Okay, okay," he says, rubbing his fingers into his temples, like he's trying to stimulate his brain. "I think I might have a plan. It hopefully won't land me in Guantánamo or you in a coffin. Follow my lead."

"Wait," I say. "Are you going to pretend to have diarrhea and ask to use the bathroom?"

"No," he says. "Maybe. Yes. So what? You have a better plan?"

I find myself thinking: *What would Dad do?* He was the master at winning people over, usually just by charming the crap out of them. Do I have that in me? Could I ever be the man he was? I start to think of what to say when I see the doorman distracted, chatting with one of the beautiful women who seem to be in such large abundance.

"Screw charm, let's run!" I whisper-scream, grabbing Anoop by the backpack and stealthily sprinting past the doorman. He barely turns his head as we slip through the door into the lobby. Thank you, the power of the New York hottie.

"We're in!" Anoop says. "I can't believe it!"

I can't believe it either. The first thing I see is a sign. It reads: ENTERING THIS BUILDING WITHOUT PERMISSION OF A TENANT IS CONSIDERED BREAKING AND ENTERING UNDER CITY LAW.

"Oops," Anoop says.

"Hey, sometimes you have to break the laws to catch the bad guys," I say.

"Is that something Mr. Zant taught us on a day I wasn't there?" Anoop asks.

"That's all me," I say.

"I had no idea you were such a badass, Langman," he says.

"Pay attention, AC," I say. "You'll learn something."

The lobby of the apartment building has a high ceiling and luxurious furniture. Even the plants seem expensive. Everyone is well dressed and this is clearly a nice part of town. "I don't get why Jacques stole the coins," I say. "He obviously has his own money."

"I don't think it's about money for him," Anoop says. "I don't think it ever was. I think it's just about revenge. Like how Fran snubbed him his whole life to live with you, his second family."

"It wasn't my fault!" I say. "I was just a baby!"

"Well, also, he's crazy," Anoop says. "So there's that."

"Okay, sure, there's that," I say. "To tell you the truth, I don't even care about his motives. I just want to prove that he's the one who broke into my house and killed Toby, and then it's the police's problem or the jury's problem or whatever to figure out why he did it and what it means. I just want him behind bars so I can get some rest."

"Right on," Anoop says. "Any brilliant ideas about how we find his fingerprint?" Anoop says. "I wish these mailboxes had names instead of just apartment numbers. If there was one that said Langman, we could—"

"Dude, shut up!" I hiss.

"What?" Anoop says. I grab him by the arm and pull him behind a large potted plant.

"Dude," I say in a whisper, trying to point without looking obvious. "That's him!"

CHAPTER TWENTY-FOUR

It's hard to believe, yet undeniable. The guy striding out the door of this New York apartment building is my brother, my would-be murderer: none other than Jacques Langman. I recognize the beard from the funeral and I recognize everything else from my DNA. It's not a perfect match, of course, but he has the same big eyes, the same quick walk, the same busy hands, and the same bushy hair as my father. As me.

"That's totally him!" Anoop says. "I'd recognize that Langman nose anywhere." So, yeah, okay, there's also that. "Follow him!" Anoop barks. "Quick!"

We learned a lot in forensics about how to catch someone *after* a crime was committed. We learned a lot about investigating the scene of a crime. But we didn't exactly learn a lot about surveillance. Zant never taught us that. Let's hope I do have some good hunches and we can come up with something on the fly.

"Act casual," Anoop says, which is always bad advice. The only way you can act casual is when you feel casual. It's pretty impossible to fake it. You're like, "Hey, I'm casual," and you start doing stuff like whistling or jingling your keys, which really aren't casual gestures. "Let's just pretend we're two guys walking down the street," Anoop says.

"Um, we *are* just two guys walking down the street," I say.

"No we're not! We're two guys on the trail of a killer, only he doesn't know that we're after him, so keep it cool."

"How long do we keep following him? Until he—" I don't finish my sentence because Jacques stops quickly. Anoop and I put on the brakes and both pretend to be looking at a rather non-descript building. Jacques is just picking up a piece of garbage to toss in a nearby trash can, however, and then he quickly resumes walking.

"Did he see us?" I whisper.

"Better question: What kind of New Yorker picks up random sidewalk garbage?" Anoop asks.

"Seriously," I say.

Then Jacques stops again, this time to hand a tissue to a lady sneezing on the corner. "He is the weirdest New Yorker ever."

"Not to mention a pretty polite murderer," Anoop says.

We continue our surveillance as he continues to walk. We stay just a few paces behind him. He stops suddenly again. I assume it's because he hears the cry of a far-off dog that needs his help. He's the nicest man in New York. He's like Superman without the tights. But instead, he turns on his heel and stares right at me. I try to look away, to stare at a building, to pretend to hail a cab, to do something, anything! But it's too late.

"Hello, Mr. Langman," he says. "I'm Mr. Langman."

My heart is pounding in my chest. I can hear the blood rushing through my body. My mouth goes suddenly dry. My bladder feels suddenly full. Being scared does some strange things to you, biologically speaking. Seriously: God or Darwin or whoever is to blame for the human body—what is up with that? Why does getting scared make you have to pee? Couldn't I have a shell like a turtle? Or wings like a bird? Anything to get out of here with dry pants and a still-beating heart.

"Eh . . . oh . . . eh," is all I can stammer and for once Anoop isn't any better.

"Eee . . . eee . . . oh," he says. We're awesome. Anoop just keeps looking back and forth between the two Langmans staring at each other on this busy street, at a loss for words for presumably the first time ever.

"Do you care to explain why you're stalking me?" Jacques asks. This makes me angry enough that my voice returns.

"Oh, that's rich," I say. "You break into my house, you come to my town to try to kill me, you murder Toby Weingarten!"

On the street, a few heads turn. Even in New York, yelling about murder gets people to turn their heads. No one actually stops what they're doing. No one turns off their cell phones. No one bats an eye. No, nothing like that. But they turn their heads, which seems to mean this is a pretty big deal. Jacques doesn't seem to think so. In fact, he laughs.

"I'm sorry," he says. "I shouldn't laugh. I'm sorry that Toby Weingarten got murdered, whoever that is, but I assure you that I had nothing to do with it."

"And I guess that you didn't break into my house either," I say. "I guess you didn't climb the tree outside my house, leap onto the roof, and break into the attic to swipe the sunken treasure that is mine!"

At this, Jacques laughs again. And really I can't blame him this time. It does sound ridiculous. Plus, I'm sort of yelling. Yelling about sunken treasure. It gets the attention of a large policeman walking by. This is exactly what I wanted—the police to take

Jacques into custody—but somehow it doesn't seem right. Plus, I think about the knife Anoop is smuggling. What if the cop pats us down and *we* get arrested? My heart starts to pound. I take a deep breath.

"Everything okay here, boys?" the policeman asks. He's asking in that calm way cops have, but his powerful arms and fists look ready for action.

"Yes, Officer," Jacques says. "There just seems to be a little misunderstanding between me and my brother here." Man, it feels weird to hear him call me his *brother*. The cop sighs. Family problems, he must be thinking. Weird thought. I'm totally having a family problem with Jacques.

"A misunderstanding that could all be cleared up if Jacques here would simply allow us to compare his prints against the exemplar," Anoop says. "And if we see some unusual double-loop whorls, then you, sir, must arrest this man." He takes his fingerprinting kit out of his backpack and holds it high over his head like a boxer hoisting the championship belt. Seriously, Anoop? Seriously? You're quiet for the first time in your entire life and then you end the silence with that?

The cop shakes his head. "What's that, now?" he says. It's a fair question.

"These boys seem to think that I'm guilty of something," Jacques says. "But I certainly am not."

"Then let us take your prints," I say, trying to remain calm and quiet. "That's all I ask."

Jacques extends his hands toward me, showing all ten fingers. It's an odd gesture. It almost looks like he wants to give me a hug. The officer is now just sort of amused, maybe bemused.

Something in the "mused" family. Maybe it's a slow crime day in NYC. Maybe working in Chelsea is boring. He leans against a tree and watches as Anoop takes over.

"All you have to do, Jacques," he says, "is press your finger onto this and I'll do the rest." Jacques has been printed before, I think, remembering his police record. He knows exactly how this is done.

Anoop hands Jacques a white card from inside the fingerprinting kit. Jacques does as he is told—which, wait, doesn't seem right. That isn't something a guilty man would likely do here. What *would* he do? My head is swimming. But better not to overthink it. Just wait for the evidence, right, Mr. Zant? I don't have to wait long. Anoop's hands may have been shaking as much as my own, but he stays calm long enough to lift a perfect print. He takes the printout of the exemplar out from the kit. It is so easy to make a match. If only the prints match. Even before Anoop says anything, it is clear. His lips are pursed, his shoulders are slumped, and his head is hanging down as if he's a kid who just got beat at checkers.

"No match," he says, in a quiet voice barely audible above the thrum of traffic noise and the honking of cars. "Not even close."

Jacques smiles. And the funny thing is, it's not the smile of a killer. It's a friendly smile. A brotherly smile. Was I wrong about him the whole time? "Sorry to take your time, Officer," he says to the cop, saluting. "I think the trouble here is over."

"Okay, boys," the officer says, chuckling to himself and throwing us back a halfhearted salute. "Stay out of trouble."

It's too late for that, I think.

"I'm sorry, Guy," Jacques says. "We really have gotten off on the wrong foot here. Or perhaps the wrong finger?" He wiggles his fingers at me. Hilarious. Wait: that's like the exact opposite of the joke, but still sort of the same exact joke, I made back in Forensics Squad. The game is a-finger? Before I can continue to think about whether or not the hilarious Langman sense of humor is genetic, Jacques thrusts his hand toward Anoop. His eyes are still on me. "Please introduce me to your fingerprinting friend, and please let me buy you guys a coffee. Do you drink coffee? I'm sorry, I don't have kids. I don't really know any young people. Do boys your age drink coffee?"

"I'm Anoop Chattopadhyay," Anoop says. "And I would love a double-tall soy latte."

"I'm Guy Langman," I say. "And I'll have a hot chocolate with extra marshmallows."

"That's too weird!" Jacques says. "I always order hot cocoa too. I'm sorry, but I just can't get behind the yuppie coffee-drink thing. No offense, Anoop." Man, this might be the weirdest thing I've ever thought, but I think I love Jacques Langman right now.

"Well, we can't take too long," Anoop mutters. "Busy day, you know . . ."

Jacques leads us into a small coffee shop—there are about a thousand of them in this part of the city—and orders our drinks from the counter while we find seats in the crowded shop. Anoop is whispering to me from our booth: "Dude, I think there is still some way . . . I mean, he could have planted the fingerprints, or something . . ."

"Let it go," I say, holding up my hand and breathing a literal sigh of relief. "Jacques Langman is not our suspect. He's my brother." Anoop rolls his eyes.

"Don't forget the matter of his criminal record," he says, at the worst possible moment. Because Jacques is back within earshot, delivering our steaming mugs.

"Oh, I see you did your research," Jacques says. "I'm impressed."

"Yeah, well, we have a friend who is kind of a hacker. He looked you up and got the address and, yeah, well, there was also something about assault with a deadly weapon, and we thought that since you were in Berry Ridge for the funeral and then the coins went missing and this good-looking guy who looked like me from North Berry Ridge ended up dead on the golf course . . ." I realize I'm babbling.

"Okay," Jacques says, softly blowing on his hot chocolate and flashing a smile so Fran-familiar it hurts. "You're going to have to explain all that, because it doesn't really make any sense. But I'll go first. There are a million ways to get an 'assault with a deadly weapon' charge on your record. And mine is probably the dumbest of all time . . ."

"They all have one thing in common, though," Anoop mutters. "The whole deadly weapon thing. Two things, really. Also the assault."

"The deadly weapon with which I assaulted Officer Leo Humbolt of Easton, Pennsylvania," Jacques says, "was a beer bottle." I look over at Anoop and see his face twisted into the same skeptical expression I feel I must be wearing. "It's true," Jacques says. "The year was 1984. A very political year. I was young, and maybe sort of crazy. I went to an anti–Ronald Reagan rally in Pennsylvania . . . Do you know who Ronald Reagan was?"

"Dude, Guy was just quoting the Monroe Doctrine," Anoop

says. "And I got a perfect score on my SATs. I think we know who Ronald Reagan was."

"Pardon me," Jacques says. "I don't know what kids know."

"We're not kids," I say. It feels good to say it, though the statement is perhaps undermined by the marshmallows stuck to my lip.

Jacques pauses for a second. "It's hard for me not to think of you that way," he says. His voice trails off. Then he continues his story of Reagan-era cop-fighting. "Well, I was at a protest. It was a political time for a number of reasons. I was young. The cops were way out of line, I know that. I threw a beer bottle. It hit Officer Humbolt. The rest is, as they say, history."

Is this the truth?

"Did you go to jail?" Anoop asks.

"No, he got off," I say.

"That's not *quite* right," he says. "But I am impressed with your research. I refused to rat on the others at the protest, so they came up with the harshest charge they could come up with. But Dad knew a good lawyer and I ended up going to rehab."

"Were you on drugs?"

"Um, it was the 1980s."

"Fair enough," I say, though I don't quite know what that means. Was everyone high in the 1980s? That would explain a lot of the hairstyles, and quite a bit of the music.

"The true tragedy of that day was the wedge it drove between me and Dad," Jacques says. "He was, as you probably know, quite stubborn. He wanted me to change everything about my life. Take drug tests on a regular basis. Change my major. I refused, and, well, we grew apart. Months turned into years and eventually . . ." His gesture means "you." I mean "me." *I* happened.

We sit and sip from our mugs in silence for a moment. Well, not total silence. There is the clatter of dishes, the chatter of a thousand conversations, and the traffic noise still audible from outside. Somewhere a siren screams. There are a million things happening at once in this city, in this world, but nothing matters more than this. Nothing matters more than family.

"I'm not quite sure I understand why hitting a policeman with a beer bottle would make Dad so angry," I say. "It seems like the kind of thing he'd do himself. And I don't think he really cared about drugs. He definitely smoked pot—how else could he justify his wardrobe, not to mention his beard?"

Jacques laughs. His eyes twinkle. "He used to drive my mom nuts with a choice Hawaiian shirt. It had, like, guitars and boobs all over it."

"He drove my mom nuts with that too! We still have it. I wore it the other day."

"I have pictures!" Anoop butts in, flipping through his phone, showing Jacques the pictures of me on the day we went to the golf course. I can't believe I thought Jacques was trying to kill me. We all laugh. I'm still feeling confused.

"But what—he wanted you to change your major? From what to what?"

"From theater," Jacques said. "To . . . anything."

"Dad hates theater?"

Anoop interrupts. "Um, Guy, sorry to interrupt again."

"No you're not."

"No, not really," Anoop sighs.

"I like him," Jacques says.

Anoop continues. "But what Jacques means is that, if I may be so bold, Fran wasn't cool with Jacques's lifestyle."

"I don't get it."

"I guess," Jacques says, "the nose is hereditary, but the gaydar isn't."

Anoop laughs. I'm still a little confused. "It's true," Jacques says. "I am a gay man. My father—that is to say, *our* father—may have made peace with that at some time, but in 1984 he was not a fan."

My heart starts to sink, like the last marshmallow to the bottom of the cup. "I'm so sorry," I say. I'm not sure why I'm apologizing, but I don't know what else to say. Jacques is so freaking cool. How could anyone—more important, how could *Dad*—care if he was gay or not? I feel like crying.

"Oh, I don't blame you," he says. "Anymore." He smiles. "I had a lot of anger toward Dad. He had a lot of good, but also a lot of bad in him. Just like everyone, I suppose. He was large, he contained multitudes."

"Hey, Walt Whitman!" I say. "Dad loved him."

"You did a great job with the reading at the funeral," Jacques says. "I was just a little jealous. Just a little."

"I'm sorry," I say. Sorry for everything.

"I don't know. Maybe it was all for the best. I ended up doing okay for myself. Did he ever talk about me?"

"No," I say, in barely a whisper. "I'm sorry."

"Please don't be. All is forgiven. The only reason to carry baggage," he says, "is if you're a fool."

"Or you work at the airport," I say, finishing the line. Dad had said it many times. Jacques smiles.

"Well," he says, checking the time on his watch. "I know

you have a bus to catch. It was nice to meet you, Guy Langman," he says. "And Anoop of the double-tall soy latte and perfect SATs. Let's hang out again sometime. You know where to
find me."

"We sure do," I say. "We sure do."

CHAPTER TWENTY-FIVE

Anoop and I spend most of the bus ride home doing two things: (1) saying "WTF was that?" over and over again, and (2) sleeping. But mostly saying "WTF was that?" Jacques turns out to be a nice guy? It so wasn't right that Dad cut him out of his life. I mean, I know there are always two sides to every story. Unless, I guess, one of the sides is a dead man. But how could Dad possibly explain his actions? Was there a good reason for Dad acting the way he did? I can't think of any. It was just unfair. And not very much like the Fran Langman I knew. Maybe Dad mellowed with age. Maybe he cared less. It is a lot to think about. It makes me so angry that Dad acted so terribly. And it makes me so angry that he kept secrets from me. But mostly all this new information makes me sad because the one person I want to talk about it with will never be able to answer my questions.

And what does this mean for our investigation? We're no closer to figuring out who broke into my house or how Toby Weingarten died. WTF indeed.

After the bus deposits us safely back in the land of Berry Ridge and Anoop takes me home, I feel like I still need to talk about it. In a day of firsts, why not another? I call Maureen. I start by composing a text, then deleting it a hundred times. Sometimes you can't find a way to squeeze what you are feeling into a text message. Sometimes there is the need for the mouth-words. The phone rings two times.

"Guy!" Maureen says. "I'm so glad you called! I have some . . . well, I'm not sure if it's good news or bad news. It's just news."

"Most of the time life doesn't break down into a good-news, bad-news situation anyway. I'm okay with that," I say. "Most news is just weird. I have some weird news myself."

"Is it about Toby?"

"No," I say. "Well, maybe. I don't know. You go." I cough. "Go on," I say.

"I'm pretty sure it *was* suicide," she says.

"What? How do you know?"

"He sort of . . . he sort of left a note."

"No one mentioned a note! They looked everywhere!"

"Not a physical note. Online. He left it on JerseyGoths."

"Um, that doesn't make any sense. Aren't the Gothics all girls?"

Maureen laughs. "I'm sorry. It's not funny. Just—'the Gothics'? You sound like my grandmother."

"Shut up," I say. But I don't say it mean. "Toby seemed like just a regular guy, not a practitioner of the Gothic lifestyle." I say it super-dorky on purpose. Just teasing. Flirting? Shut up.

"Lots of 'regular guys' have dark sides, Guy. And, no, it's not just girls. Dudes post on there sometimes. There's no real rule against it . . ." Some of them are creeps. Some of them are okay. Toby was okay. I actually knew him. I mean, I talked to him, once or twice on there. I just never knew it was him, if you know what I mean. I knew his screen name, but it wasn't until I did some digging tonight that I figured out it was him!"

"Did he seem sad?"

"Um, yeah. I mean, everyone on there does. That's what we all have in common."

"Why are you so sad, Maureen Fields?" I ask. I don't know why. It just comes out.

"I don't even know that I am anymore," she says with a giggle. "But don't tell the Gothics."

"Your secret shame of being happy sometimes is safe with me," I say. "But what was up with Toby? Soft signs of suicide?"

"What?" she says.

"That's something I read. Sometimes there is nothing obvious, nothing *overt*, but sometimes when they dig into the person's life, there are hints. Clues. Soft signs of suicide."

"I should write that down," she says. "You're a poet, Guy Langman."

"I'm also confused," I say.

"Aren't we all?"

"I think so," I say. "If being sort of sad and pissed off and confused are soft signs of suicide, it's a wonder any of us are alive."

"Yeah," she says. Then she's quiet for a moment. I just hear her breathing and the scrape of her pen. Black ink on black paper, no doubt.

"But I'm, like, specifically confused about something," I say. "This note is legit?"

"I'm pretty sure," she says. "A few girls on there knew him really well. His last post was real upsetting stuff. And then nothing since the day Toby died. Not a peep. He hasn't been this quiet on there in years. I guess when he saw that electrical tower he wandered off from the group, climbed it, and jumped. He'd probably climbed that tree thinking the same, but couldn't go through with it. A little while later . . . he did."

"Man," I say, feeling so sad for Toby. "It really is sad. Did he know he was going to do it? If you want to die, how do you still go about your day? Get up. Eat breakfast. Get dressed. Go on the Forensics Squad trip. And then . . ."

"Is that what you're confused about, Guy?" she says.

"Well, um, yeah, that. But also—how did the same fingerprints get on Toby's wallet and my wall? It wasn't my half brother. Anoop and I shot that theory down today."

"You did?" she asks. So I tell her all about it. She seems a little bummed that I went to the city without her. I tell her I'll take her sometime. Shut up.

"Okay, I've been thinking about that too," she says.

"Any theories?"

"Just that we need to expand the suspect list."

"Well, who the hell else would have been up there? No one else knew about those coins."

"No one?"

"Well, Anoop knew," I say. There is another pause. This time I don't even hear the pen on paper. This time I just hear the breathing. "No way," I say. "No freaking way."

"Think about it," she says. "His prints *would* be on the wallet. He was the one who found it."

"I was the one who found it!"

"Well, whatever. He obviously touched it. He took it back to his house."

"He was wearing rubber gloves."

"Are you sure?"

"Pretty sure . . ."

"Well anyway, he took the thing home. He could have placed a print on there at any time."

"He put it in an evidence Baggie. You saw that."

"Yeah, we all saw that. But no one saw what he did with it when he had it at home." My heart was beating really fast. Would Anoop really do that? Why?

"It doesn't make any sense," I say.

"It makes perfect sense," she says. "You were fighting with Anoop anyway. He knew about those coins. How much did you say they were worth?"

"A lot."

"Enough for a new car? You know how people make fun of Anoop's car all the time. And he's got his rich new girl to impress . . ."

"People make fun of the AC Machine? I mean, I know I do, but I didn't know other people did."

"Okay, by 'people' I meant you."

"Fair enough. But have you seen that thing? What is he, an algebra teacher? Okay, okay. But he would, what, break in to steal the coins and sell them for a new car? Then help me lift the prints on the attic wall, knowing they would be his own?"

"Well, he had to do it. TK was there with you. Plus, you know what Mr. Zant would say. Prints don't mean anything unless you have something to compare them to. It wouldn't mean anything to have his prints."

"So he'd plant his own prints on the wallet just to make me think that the break-in wasn't him?"

"Yeah. He knew he could throw you off the trail. If he put the print on the wallet, you'd see that and match it to the window print and you'd really think it was Jacques!"

"Anoop is smart," I say. "But that's, like, evil genius smart. I think you lost me halfway through."

"Thank you," she says.

"That wasn't a compliment."

"It kinda was. You kinda said I was an evil genius."

"I said *Anoop* was an evil genius."

"But I figured it out, so that sort of makes me an evil genius too."

"Fine, everyone around here is an evil genius. What do we do now?

"That's the million-dollar question," she says. "Too bad you're not an evil genius too."

"I guess we could wait and see if Anoop shows up at school with a shiny new Lexus or something."

"By then it would be too late. The coins would be sold and it would be impossible to get them back, even though they are stolen property."

"I can't believe Anoop would do this to me," I say. "I literally cannot believe it. It makes no sense. He's been so into the investigation, besides everything else. Why would he drag me into the city? Just to throw me off his trail?"

"Maybe."

"But he had to know that Jacques's fingerprints would prove it *wasn't* him."

"Who knows? Maybe Anoop is crazy. What do we really know about him?"

"I've known him my whole life. I know he used to watch *Dora the Explorer* until he was way too old for it. I know he cried on his ninth birthday because his neighbor Mark Conrad went to Don Rossini's party instead. I know his 'if I had to make out with a man' choice is Derek Jeter. I know everything about him."

"Except for if he stole your treasure."

"No," I begin to say. "There is no way—"

"You know," she says. "There is a way we could find out."

"There is?"

"Yeah," she says. "I was reading a book about forensics projects—"

"You have got to be kidding me."

"Get over it, Guy. Yes, I'm a huge nerd. Since we're going to be friends, it will be just a lot easier if you accept that."

"We're going to be friends? When? Was there a memo or an email that went out or something? I don't remember agreeing to—"

"Shut up, Guy. We're totally friends. And the book had a project for building a lie detector."

"What?"

"Yeah, it's actually not all that hard to build. I talked to TK about it. He said he has all the parts you'd need."

"What is TK's deal, anyway?"

"I don't know. Talk about evil genius. He's nice, though."

"Okay, so TK builds this lie detector. I can't imagine how we get Anoop to take it."

"Well, obviously we don't just come out and say 'Hey, Anoop, we want to see if you stole thirty thousand dollars' worth of treasure from Guy's house, so come over and let us strap you to this lie detector TK made with some crap from his garage.'"

"Okay, what then?"

"You leave that up to me, Guy Langman," she says. "I shall use my feminine wiles."

"Feminine wiles? When did you get those?"

"Shut up, Guy Langman. I'll talk to you later." She hangs up sort of quickly. Dad always called this the Irish good-bye. I'm not sure why. But instead of just lingering all awkward at the end of a conversation or something, I guess the Irish just run out of there. Is Maureen Fields Irish? And, okay, I have some bigger questions simmering here. Is there any possible way that Anoop stole the coins? And if poor Toby really jumped to his death and it *wasn't* Anoop who stole the coins, then who was it? And hey, Maureen Fields is fun to talk to *and* she apparently has feminine wiles. That being the case, I guess anything's possible.

CHAPTER TWENTY-SIX

Sure enough, the next meeting of the unofficial Forensics Squad, held at Langman Manor, features TK and his homemade lie detector. We're assembled in the great room again. Raquel and TK. Me and Maureen. And sure enough, Anoop is here, looking clueless. Maureen's feminine wiles surely did the trick.

"Thanks for coming, everyone," Maureen says. Wily. "As I told you all, there is some very important news about the case." Mutter, mutter, mutter. "Toby Weingarten did not kill himself. Toby Weingarten was murdered." Gasp, gasp, gasp. I'm just confused. Didn't she just call me and tell me it *was* suicide? Feminine wiles sure are wily.

"I don't get it," Anoop says. "How can you know that?"

"Let's just say I have some inside information," she says. "I think it was someone on his team from North Berry Ridge who did it."

"Stupid North Berry Ridge jerks," I say reflexively.

"Yeah," TK says. "Exactly. And I know how we're going to catch them. I'm going to get Zant to set up a rematch so we can see who is the rightful owner of Sherlock's Glass. The challenge will be to create a working lie detector, which, as luck would have it, I've already done." TK takes out his lie detector. It's a wooden box about the size of a shoe box, dotted with lights and full of wires sticking out in all directions. He shrugs. "It just takes a few transistors, a capacitor, some LEDs, about five regular resistors, and a variable resistor."

"Oh yeah?" I say. I've figured out that this whole thing is a ruse. There is no rematch. Maureen just said that Toby was murdered to set this up. This is just an excuse to make Anoop wear the lie detector. Oh yeah, I get it. Total masculine wiles.

"It will have to be adjusted for each person who uses it," TK says. "And if we want to catch the North Berry Ridge jerk who killed Toby, we need to make sure it works correctly. That's where you guys come in. I'm hoping you can help me out."

TK is about to ask Anoop to be the first volunteer when Raquel volunteers. "I like this!" she says. Um, okay. Her wiles are all out of whack. "Do me first," she says. Everyone snickers a little. TK and Maureen share a look. This wasn't part of the plan. But Maureen smiles and plays along.

"Go ahead," she says. "Yeah, totally. Go for it." TK applies the sensors to her hand and tweaks some settings. Maureen asks some questions. "Okay, would you ever go out with Guy?"

"Um, no," she says.

"True statement," TK says.

Why did she have to ask that?

"Um, does anyone else want to try this?" TK asks. "Anoop?"

"Oh, no," Anoop says. "You aren't getting me hooked up to that thing. No offense, TK, but until you actually get the PhD, I'm not wearing some device you built out of crap in your garage. I don't need to get electrocuted for this."

"You do need electrolysis for this," I say, pointing to my forehead. Everyone looks at me weird. "Electrolysis. It's, like, hair removal—come on, people," I say. "For the unibrow? Never mind."

Anoop gives me an angry look. And okay, dumb joke, but bigger point: He won't do it! What is he trying to hide? Are his own Anoopian wiles telling him that something is up?

"It's totally safe," TK says. "I assure you."

"Yeah," Raquel says in a flirty voice. "It does not hurt at all." She shows him the spot on her fingers where the pads had touched. "Why not try it on, Noopie?"

Okay, Noopie? How can he refuse? He's probably setting himself up to be convicted of stealing his best friend's treasure, but he doesn't even care, because Raquel is calling him Noopie. After a few minutes of fiddling with the diodes or whatever, TK announces that we can begin the interrogation of the Bengal Tiger.

Maureen, clearly enjoying the power this has given her, begins asking Anoop some questions. At first they are the basic ones, just to get obvious yes-or-no answers from Anoop to help TK determine the accuracy of the device. "Are you Indian? Is Guy your boyfriend? What is pi to the first eight digits after the decimal?" (That'd be yes, no, and 3.14159265, if you're playing along at home.)

Then she asks him what *he* probably thinks is another easy, pointless question. Wily.

"Did you steal Guy's dad's treasure?"

"Um, no," he says.

"Is that correct?" she asks TK.

"Unless my device is mistaken, that is a true statement," he says.

"Your stupid device *is* mistaken!" I yell.

"Um, what?" Anoop says. He laughs. I'm not laughing, though.

"Did we seriously think TK could build a working lie detector?

No offense, TK, but that's ridiculous. It's clear that Anoop took the treasure! It's clear that he wanted a fancy car to impress Raquel or someone, and since we were fighting, you broke into my house and stole the treasure!" I can't believe I'm saying the word "treasure" so many times. My life has gotten seriously weird.

"I can't believe you are accusing me of this," Anoop says.

"That doesn't sound like a denial," Maureen says.

"Did *you* put him up to this?" Anoop asks.

"I'm just saying."

"Sure," Anoop says. "Everyone is always *just saying* things. After everything we've been through, I cannot believe this. What else are you saying? That I killed that kid?"

"No," I say. "No way. No one is saying that. We're just saying that maybe you felt like you really needed some money, and since we were fighting . . . Listen, Toby's death was not murder. I'm just saying you can give the coins back and we can all retire from our careers in crime-solving."

"There is just one problem with that theory," Anoop says. "I didn't steal the stupid coins! Guy, we've been friends our whole lives. You think I would break into your house? Fine—put me back on the lie detector. Better yet, take my prints. They're right here." He shoves his hand in my face. I flinch. Is he going to hit me? "Better yet, check this." He reaches into his notebook and pulls out the card from the first day of Forensics Squad.

He takes out the magnifying glass from the kit. The card clearly says AC on the back. And on the front . . . a loop-and-ridge pattern clearly different from the other one. Anoop's print is nothing like the one we've been searching for. It doesn't match Anoop's, it doesn't match Jacques Langman's, it doesn't match anyone's. It doesn't make any sense. How could the same fingerprint end up on the wallet of Toby Weingarten and the window of Guy Langman? There's no link. None whatsoever. Unless . . .

"Anoop," I say. "I'm so sorry." I really am so sorry. What was I thinking? Stupid Maureen Fields was messing with my head. I keep babbling. "I'm so, so sorry," I say. "Sorry we doubted you. I'm also sorry I told Maureen your 'if I had to make out with a man' choice is Derek Jeter. And now I've told the entire room. Jeter *is* sort of handsome, I'll give you that."

"Guy," Anoop says, his face darkening and his fists curling up. Maybe he really is going to hit me? "What the hell are you talking about?"

"I like Jeter too," Raquel says. "But Anoop is cuter." *Ewwww.* But hey, actually that was nice of you, Raquel. Divert Anoop with some praise. Save me from getting punched.

"Anoop," I say, pointing to the cards from the first day of Forensics Squad that spilled out of his notebook. "Pass me the one labeled 'HD.'" He relaxes his fist enough to pick up the card. He still sort of looks like he wants to kill me, but he passes it my way.

"The magnifying glass, please." He hands it over. "Just as I thought," I say, checking out the fingerprint of one Hairston Danforth III. "Some very unusual double-loop whorls."

Anoop retrieves the exemplar from our previous efforts—the print that was on both the wallet of Toby Weingarten and my wall. I hand him Hairston's card. I don't have to compare the two. I know that they are a match.

"Holy crap," Anoop says, which just about sums it up. He holds the magnifying glass up to Hairston's print. Then back and forth, comparing it to our exemplar. "It's a perfect match. Hairston Danforth killed Toby Weingarten."

At this Maureen, TK, and I laugh. "Sorry," Maureen says. "It's really not funny. But Toby wasn't murdered. It was suicide."

"Hilarious?" Anoop says.

"I know," TK says. "It really isn't funny. It's just that Maureen set this thing up to get you here. Hairston is a thief, but he's not a murderer."

"You really thought I stole your freaking coins after everything we've been through, Guy Langman?" Anoop says. "I really ought to kick your ass."

"But I think you have other plans," I say, looking over at Raquel and winking.

"Hells to the yeah," he says. "I'm going over to Hairston Danforth's house and demanding your coins back. And demanding that he tell us how he even knew about them. And how his prints ended up on Toby's wallet. Because I am a good friend even to those who don't deserve it."

"I don't deserve it, Noopie," I say, feeling like I really don't. "But I can answer at least some of that. I never tell anyone about those coins, but I was talking to Hairston one day . . . I was feeling sad or weird or whatever. I just kept talking. Accidentally blurted it out. I didn't really believe that he was a klepto."

"Totally is," TK says.

"Yeah," I say. "And he actually mentioned that he had some North Berry Ridge friends. He probably knew Toby. Probably tried to steal his wallet."

"Yup," Maureen says. "That's what I was thinking."

"Is this posse ready to roll?" Anoop says. "I'm ready to kick some ass. We could all go over there with you. Blow this bitch up in a commando-style Forensics Squad smackdown."

"I could rig up some climbing ropes and we could rappel down the side of his house, then kick in the windows with our feet, SWAT-team style," TK says.

"That sounds totally awesome," I say, because it does. "But I'm not entirely sure it's necessary. I'm just going to go over there. No fisticuffs. We'll have a talk. We'll figure things out." *Did I say "fisticuffs"?*

"You're a bigger man than I, Guy Langman," Anoop says.

"That's what your mother says," I say. We laugh. Ah, mother jokes. Life, it seems, is getting normal again.

CHAPTER TWENTY-SEVEN

Here's the plan: I show up at Hairston's house with a paper bag. He'll say, "Oh, is that my vintage *Playboy* in there?" And I'll say, "No, you will find that this bag does not contain any *Playboys*." And he'll say, "Oh, what does it contain?" And I'll say, "Look closely and you will find that it contains . . . my fist!" And then my hand smashes through the empty paper bag and hammers him in the nose. Blood everywhere. Ha-ha, yeah! Take that, Hairston, you thieving multi-use hand tool! That's what you get for breaking into my house and stealing my treasure!

Okay, wait, I promised no fisticuffs. And I'm not really the fisticuffs type, anyway. I'm just going to go over there and talk to him, man-to-man. I know Dad always wanted me to be the fisticuffs type, but it's starting to sink in that not everything he said was brilliant. Not every action he did was perfect. As it says in the Bible, "All dudes fuck up sometimes. Get over it." (Okay, I only ever skimmed the Bible.) But I feel like Dad would be proud that I'm handling this on my own, with dignity and firm honor. I'll present Hairston with some solid evidence and there's no way he can deny it. And if he tries, well, I'm not totally ruling out punching him in the balls.

Hairston's address is easy enough to find—right there in the phone book. I sort of knew whereabouts it was anyway—a neighborhood you can walk to from mine—not that I've ever ventured over there. No one did, really. I'm feeling sort of bad for old Penis-Head, which is the wrong frame of mind to begin a manly confrontation. I walk over there, slowly cruising up and down the wide streets, past the beautiful lawns and enormous houses. How can so much weird shit go down in a place like this?

I get to Hairston's place and no, it doesn't have a sign out front announcing it as "Danforth Manor" or "Casa de Penis-Head," but it really is a mansion with a gate out front and everything. Why would Hairston steal? Is he really a drug addict? My stomach sinks. What if he already sold the coins for drug money? Or for whatever type of money? The coins could be gone. Gone. Gone. Gone. Every link to my father feels sacred. I can't stand the idea of losing any of it . . . Plus, given the sad state of the Langman finances, that could be my college tuition right there. (Yeah, yeah, I'm getting around to applying. Don't tell Anoop, though. He might wet himself.)

To get past the gate, you have to ring a buzzer. I press the small silver button and after a few seconds recognize the sleepy voice coming out of a speaker. It's like being at a fast-food restaurant. "Hello," he says.

"Yeah, I'll have a cheeseburger and a seasoned curly fries," I say. I can't help it. It really feels like a drive-thru.

"Piss off," he says.

"Dude, it's Guy Langman!" I yell, before he can break the connection. He probably thinks I'm some kid playing a prank.

"I know," he says. "There's a camera. I can see who it is. That's why I said 'Piss off.' "

"What did I ever do to you?" I yell. When I pictured this

conversation going down, I didn't picture it being an argument with a drive-thru speaker and a hidden camera.

"I don't know," he says after a long while. Then he adds, "What do you want?"

"Can I come in?" I ask.

"Are you alone?"

"Yes," I say, feeling sort of creeped out that he asked. "Just me. Left the troops back at the barracks."

He doesn't say anything, but I hear a soft click and the gate swings open. I make my way up the long, winding path to the front door, which also softly clicks open before I even have to open it.

"Sweet system," I say, as Hairston meets me in the foyer. "Doors open themselves, hidden cameras, not bad."

He shrugs. "Makes my parents feel safe leaving me here, I guess. Since they're never home."

"Away on business again?" I ask.

"Yeah," he says.

"Cool, cool."

It is then that I notice the gun.

This changes things somewhat. I'm about to confront Hairston with a crime. I'm prepared, if necessary, to go to the level of fisticuffs. But a shootout is not something I bargained for. Hairston sees me seeing the gun. It's a long old shotgun or something, sitting on a small table at the bottom of the stairs.

"You know, some of the rumors about me *are* true," he says.

"You really are an arms dealer?"

"No, not that," he says. "That's just one of my dad's toys. You know rich men and their collections."

"Well, please don't shoot me!" I say. I try to make it a joke, but really, I'm scared. It turns out that I'm scared for good reason. Hairston reaches for the gun and I leap into action. I grab him sort of awkwardly by the shoulders and he elbows me in the stomach. It hurts and I grunt, but I don't let go. I adjust my grip and end up securing him in a side headlock. I elbow him in the ear somehow.

"Let go of me!" he shrieks.

"No way. Not until you put down the gun."

"Never!" he says.

I twist his head harder, and am able to kick the gun out of his hand while still holding him in a headlock. The gun clatters to the floor, echoing on the hardwood. I chuck him across the room and dive for the gun. I grab it and point it at Hairston.

"Oh my God, Hairston. You really were going to kill me."

"Dude, it's a two-hundred-year-old musket," he says, rubbing his ear. "I don't even think it works. It doesn't even have bullets, or musket balls or whatever. And it takes forever to load. How did we even win the Revolutionary War?"

"Um, I really am not sure?" I say. Still, I keep the gun pointed at him. "But I'm guessing you know why I'm here. Speaking of old men and their collections."

"Yeah," he says.

"Why did you steal my coins?"

Silence. Then he sighs.

"I knew I shouldn't have gone to that stupid Forensics Squad," he says. "Terrible idea for a thief to let someone get their prints on file."

I repeat the question. I still have the gun pointed at him, even though I know it doesn't work.

"Put the gun down," he says. He gives me a totally blank look. He's good, I'll give him that much. A real stone-faced Penis-Head.

"You'll explain all this to me?" I say.

"Sure," he says. "Fine. I'm sorry. I really am. I have this problem . . . I don't know why I take things. I don't need the money. Dr. Waters says it's just a power thing."

"Hey, you go to Dr. Waters too?" I ask.

"You go there?"

"Yeah. My mom made me go after my dad died. Dr. Waters is okay. I don't love it or anything."

"Yeah, Dr. Waters is okay. I think she's right about the power thing. I feel so powerless or whatever in most of my life that I do this to control the situation. The more difficult the theft, the more I'm drawn toward it. I've started picking pockets too. I'm weirdly good at it. Dr. Waters says it's a bad sign that I'm stealing from people. Funny thing is, one time I did it right in her office. I stole some North Berry Ridge kid's wallet right in her waiting room. Her secretary caught me, though, and I had to give it back . . ."

I jump up. "Voilà!"

"Don't check your wallet, Guy, I didn't take it, I promise."

"No," I say. "It's not that. Was the North Berry Ridge kid Toby Weingarten?"

"Who?"

"That's the kid who, uh, killed himself at the golf course when we were doing our forensics project."

"Oh yeah, now that you mention it, his face did look familiar when I saw it on the news . . . Yeah, I think it was him."

"I know."

"I didn't kill him, though, if that's what people are saying."

"I know that," I say.

"I totally remember it now. I don't think he even noticed that I took his wallet until the secretary pointed it out. She made me give it back, but I had already emptied the contents into my pocket. No one even noticed. I'm good."

"He was pretty messed up. And you *are* a really good thief."

"Thank you, thank you. Now I just need to work on finding a less, you know, illegal skill set."

"You'll get there, Hairston. I never thought I'd be good at anything, and look at me—tracking down killers, identifying whorls, dusting for prints . . ."

"Except, you know, there weren't really any killers. Kind of a weird mystery."

"Right, well . . . you know, life itself is a mystery sometimes. It's up to all of us to solve it."

"You're deep, Guy Langman," he says. "Is that from your sad journal?"

"No. Shut up."

"So I'll go get the coins. I have them upstairs."

"You still want Lisa Baker?" I ask, feeling generous.

"You've moved on from analog to digital porn?" he asks.

"Hairston, I've moved on from analog porn to reality porn," I say.

"Wait, what? You've become a porn star?"

"No, I mean, she's just, it's that, I mean—we haven't even held hands yet. I don't know why I said that. It sounded a lot less gross in my head. Forget it. I just mean, there might be a girl I like. A real girl. Born in recent decades, not a seventy-year-old lady who took her top off for money amidst articles about Norman Thomas, world's worst presidential candidate. Nothing against Lisa Baker, of course."

"You read the articles?"

"Totally. Some good stuff in there. I totally know the best places to ski in Europe now. You know, in 1966. Now if we only had skis."

"And a time machine."

"Ha-ha. You're all right, Hairston. You're all right." I realize that this is a strange thing to say to a dude with whom I so recently had fisticuffs, but he's okay.

He comes back down in a second and my heart soars as I see the old cigar box. "So listen, Guy, I'm really sorry. Thanks for not calling the police or anything."

"No problem, Hair-Bear. Just, you know, keep seeing Dr. Waters. Tell that Slippery Rock diploma and the fish that GL says howdy."

"You don't think you'll be going back?"

"You know, Hair-Bear, I don't think I will. Fifth stage, here I come . . ."

"What is the fifth stage, a bar or something like that?"

"Something like that, Hair. Something like that."

CHAPTER TWENTY-EIGHT

Maureen, TK, and I are at my house again. Just hanging out. Anoop and Raquel are off drinking double-tall soy lattes or whatever. Forensics Squad is over, disbanded. Soon the school year will be over too. Then summer vacation and—oh man—senior year.

"I am really bummed, though," I say. I'm filling them in on how I confronted Hairston to get my coins back. I'm showing TK the headlock. It's pretty fierce. I leave out the part about the Lisa Baker mag. No need exactly to bring that up.

"It did go okay," I say. "Only bummer is that I didn't get a chance to deliver an action-hero zinger. I have lots of good lines ready."

"Oh, I know you do," Maureen says.

"You should have met him in Zant's room—you could have gone with, 'There's something *fishy* going on here,'" TK says.

"I already used that one earlier. Like eight times."

"Looks like you're a *fish* out of water?" he suggests.

"Meh," I say. But then I get excited about something. I had been trying to figure out what kind of music I really like, inspired by Maureen's making fun of me. I had done some searching online and came across a band called the Dead Milkmen who I clicked on just because the name is funny. They had a song called "Swordfish!" The lyric is "I believe in swordfish" for some absurd reason.

"How about if I said, 'I believe in swordfish,' like the Dead Milkmen song?" I say.

"You know about the Dead Milkmen?" Maureen says, cocking an eyebrow, obviously impressed.

"Yeah!" I say. "I've been, you know, trying to find myself or whatever."

"Let me know what you find," she says, and punches me in the arm. But then she adds, "Most people aren't going to know who the Dead Milkmen are, so I don't know if it really counts as a quality quip. Count me as impressed, though."

"Yeah," I say.

"Hey, maybe," Maureen says, getting really excited, "you could have pretended like you were at a restaurant and said: 'Waiter, I'll have the fish!' And then stabbed him and added, 'The swordfish.'"

I laughed. "Yeah! That could work."

"I'm going to get going," TK says. "Let you two have some time together."

"Why would we want that?" I say, suddenly nervous.

TK rolls his eyes. "Someday, that Guy becomes a man. And someday that Guy takes your hand," he says.

"Omigod, you read those?!" she says. "I'm so embarrassed!"

"Don't be," I say.

"You read it too?" she says, blushing hard. "It's so emo."

"They're on the Internet, Maureen. Not exactly a secret," TK says.

"They are sweet. I've been doing some writing lately too, you know," I say.

"Will you share it with me?" she asks.

"I will," I say. "I will."

Well, damn, it's all on the table now. TK bids us adieu. I'm alone with Maureen. Um, what to do now? I break out my notebook. It's not black ink on black paper. Nothing that dramatic. Just regular pen and paper. I show her the stuff I had written about my dad, even the embarrassing parts, which is pretty much all of it. The book started out as a collection of things Dad said, then became a biography, then it's just my sad journal. It is weird, sitting there in the room with her, watching her read that notebook. It is like letting someone into my brain. It feels wrong, but right at the same time, if that makes any sense. She reads in silence for a long, long time.

"We need to burn this," she says.

"That bad?" I ask.

"No! Not bad at all! You are a good writer, Guy, really good."

"So good that it, my only written work, needs to be incinerated?"

"It would be the perfect gesture. We burn it and pour the ashes over his grave."

"Um, is this some sort of weird Goth thing?"

"It's a human thing, turd. It will be the perfect way to say good-bye."

"I'm not sure I want to say good-bye."

"You *need* to say good-bye. You need to realize that the pain you feel is real and that the only way to go on living is to go on living."

"Hey, that sounds like something Dad would have said."

"You need to stop worrying about everything he ever said and instead think about the way he lived his life. And you need to realize that some of his advice was incredibly dumb."

"Hey!" I protest. It's true, though. "And he was really a jerk to my brother," I say. "I'll tell you about him sometime . . ."

"I'd like that," she says.

I pause. I pause for a long time, trying to hold the space of sixteen years, of sixty years, of a lifetime, in just a few moments. Maybe it is time to put some of this behind me. Maybe it's okay to admit that Dad pissed me off sometimes. His sick game, pretending to be dead. And it's definitely wrong how he treated Jacques. And maybe it's wrong the way Mom never let herself grieve. Maybe it's all wrong. Maybe . . .

"You're saying I need to forget the book?"

"Forget the book, Guy," she says. "Not because it's not good, because it is! But forget the book and go on with life. It's what he would have wanted."

"It's what he would have wanted."

Neither of us has a car, and this doesn't seem like the kind of mission we could ask moms or friends to drive us to. So we walk. It is a long walk. At first we talk. She asks me about Raquel, totally smoothly working it into the conversation. "Who cares?" I say. Anoop and Raquel are a thing, or whatever. And maybe it'll work out for them. I wish him the best of luck.

Maureen and I reach the narrow shoulder of the busy main road through Berry Ridge, making it so I have to walk behind her. Single file like kindergartners on a field trip. It makes it hard to hold hands. Is that something that I want? Yes. It also makes it hard to talk. There is much to say, but somehow the silence feels comfortable too. Not that it is exactly silent. The constant grind of engine noise and the whir of passing cars fills my brain, but it still feels like I am on a mission up a mountain. Revelation is where you find it, my friends. That's a Guy Langman original.

We reach Berry Ridge Cemetery. It is bright and green and sunny. Flowers and beautiful displays. You could almost forget this is a place where dead bodies are stacked beneath the ground. I show Maureen the plot where Dad is buried. It feels so strange to be there in this private place with someone else. It is like letting a friend watch you go to the bathroom for the first time. I need to work on my metaphors, clearly.

"There it is," I say.

"Why doesn't he have an inscription on his gravestone?" she asks.

"He never wanted one."

"Really?"

"His will said he didn't need one. I never really knew why. But when I was in his room the other day, looking for golfing clothes, I think I found the reason."

"Really?"

"Yeah." I reach into my pocket. I had been carrying the piece of paper with me at all times. I read it to Maureen: "'I do not need a statue. I do not need a biography written of me. I do not need plaques hung on walls or words written in stone. The world will remember me well enough when I'm gone. Because I had sons.'" I start to cry. "Thanks, Dad," I say. I wipe my eyes. "Sorry. That's weird. I don't know. I talk to him sometimes."

"No, that's really sweet," she says, and takes my hand. Her hand is hot, and a little wet. But I like it. It feels right.

"Maybe I should tell Jacques about this. Maybe it would make him feel better," I say.

"That's really sweet of you."

"He's a pretty cool guy. I'd like for you to meet him. He made fun of Anoop's coffee."

"That earns him points in my book."

"Want to take the bus into the city someday?"

"I'd like that."

It feels like she wants me to say more, but somehow nothing more needs to be said. There is silence. Our little ritual happens in silence. I take the papers, the handwritten pages of my book, and set them on the ground. She takes a lighter out of her pocket. She hands it to me so that I may do the honors. I light the corner and . . . I'm not sure what I feel. All that work! But it does seem right. Very right. It burns, the smoke pluming upward to the sky like a hand waving good-bye.

"Good-bye," I say.

"Do you talk to him a lot?" she asks.

"Yeah. All the time. And this is really weird. Sometimes he talks back. He even gives me crime-solving advice."

"So you take all the credit even though your dad does all the work?"

"That's how I roll," I say.

It gets awkward for a moment.

"Listen," she says, breaking the silence. "I brought you something." She reaches into her bag and pulls out a bundle, tied in ribbon. "Open it."

I do. It's purple and shiny and oh my Lord. "An ascot?" I ask.

"An ascot!" she says. "You said you might start wearing one. You know, just for fun or whatever . . ."

"Oh man," I say. "This is so great!" I flip it on and you know, it really feels right. Perfect.

"I'm not sure that's quite right," she says, reaching up and adjusting the ascot around my neck.

I must have gotten a strange look on my face. "What?" she asks, leaving her hand on my neck.

"Just . . . Dad," I say.

"Is he talking to you? What's he saying now?"

"Now?" I ask. "I don't know. I have to listen." I listen. It is quiet. The birds are singing. The sun is shining. The bright green trees blow in the wind. Life is going on. "He says to kiss the girl," I say.

And I do.

EPILOGUE—SENIOR YEAR

I lied before. I do go back to Dr. Waters's office, but just one last time. I'll miss you, goldfish who I named Skip. I'll miss you, comfortable leather couch. I'll miss you most of all, diploma for Slippery Rock University.

"How are you doing, Guy?" Dr. Waters asks. She's asked the question many times over the past year. Sometimes I would roll my eyes at it. *How are you doing?* That's what they pay you for? And sometimes I'd almost start crying, just knowing I'd have to talk about things I didn't want to talk about. Sometimes the question "How are you doing" is the most complicated and hardest question in the world. And sometimes, yes, I'd make a joke. I'd say stuff like "I think I've developed phobiaphobia, which is a fear of getting phobias, but maybe I don't actually have it but am just afraid of getting it? It's complicated, you know? Also, I have gas." Stuff like that.

But today I answer honestly. And the honest answer is, "I'm doing okay."

"That's wonderful to hear," Dr. Waters says. And I can tell she means it. "Have you spoken to your mother, like we talked about?"

"You know what?" I say. "I did. Mom and I have been talking *a lot* more. She took off her sunglasses, so to speak. Also literally. It was nice to see her eyes again. She opened up a bit. I opened up a bit. We ate tacos from Taco City. It was cool."

"That's wonderful," she says.

"I didn't know you loved Taco City too," I say. She laughs. Finally! I get a laugh out of Dr. Waters. Sometimes humor is a way of hiding from shit; sometimes it's just fun to make people laugh. I don't say that out loud, though. I just keep opening up. Might as well. "I figured something out. My father was not a saint. He might not have been a genius. Or he might have been. But what he was, was my father. And he left me with a lot. A whole lot. Not just some coins, not just this beautiful nose, not just a brother. He left me a great deal, even if he didn't leave me a guidebook on how to live. It's up to each of us to write our own *Rules for Living*. Each generation's guidebook is written in their own hand. The ways of the elders can only do so much." She nods. I'm deep.

"Can I read you something?" I ask. I reach into my pocket and pull out a folded printout.

"Of course you can, Guy," she says.

So I read:

"Rules for Living": The Guy Langman Story

Life is easy, my friends. Ever since the dragon
pooped the fire of earth into existence, a few rules
have existed. Scratch that. None of that is true.
Life isn't easy. But maybe it's not impossible either.
Maybe some things never change. Maybe it's always
a simple matter of stopping the bad guy, getting the
girl, making peace with your parents, and taking a
sweet bubble bath every once in a while.

I can't pretend to know all the answers, or even

some of them, but I have learned this: If you think you can avoid pain by avoiding life, you fail at both. The only way to win the game is to play the game. And okay, there's no promise you'll win, or that winning even exists. But it's the only way to be sure you don't lose.

When a stranger with a knife appears at your window (or seems to) and you think you're going to die, you can't help but get this horrible nervousness. Not just about your future, but your past. Did I spend my time the right way? Did I waste my hours with video games? But really—and okay, maybe now it's because I don't feel the metaphorical knife at my throat—I don't see it that way. All those things—games, books, even fights and even being bored—that is life. And I'll have some more, please.

So what does the future hold for Guy Langman? Will he go to college? Who are you, Anoop? Fine, I filled out the forms. Applied to a few good schools. Eugene Lang, Slippery Rock, and some others with not-as-fun names. My grades are coming back up and the extracurriculars look pretty sweet: Forensics Squad President, and a letter of recommendation from Mr. Zant.

Zant's letter makes me blush. Over and over again he said how much I've learned, how skilled I've become. He doesn't know the half of it . . . I've lifted fingerprints, outsmarted a doorman, caught a thief, confronted a villain, kissed a girl . . . Okay, no reason for the letter to mention that last part. And yeah, the villain I caught was sort of actually the nicest guy ever. And the evil cat burglar was just a messed-up kid. Oh, Hairston. All is forgiven. He isn't perfect (obviously), but he's trying. Just fumbling and bumbling along. Maybe that's all any of us can do.

Maybe you can't expect the leader of the tribe—or anyone else—to sit you down and explain the rules for living. Not now. Not anytime soon. There are no rules for living. The only leader of your tribe is you. We all lead our own tribes, of friends, parents, weird dudes at school, girls. The people you choose to love. This is your life. The world will never give you a dong bracelet. You have to reach out and take it.

ACKNOWLEDGMENTS

Imagine my surprise when I learned I'd be working with an editor who didn't even know how to spell her own last name! But even though she spells Berk with a *u* for some wacky reason, Michele Burke has been an absolutely fantastic editor (and actually a far better speller than I). Thanks so much, Michele, for your humor, wisdom, gentle guidance, and inexhaustible patience in working with me on this book. Nothing pleases me more than when I find a handwritten "ha!" in the margin of a manuscript and I know I've made you laugh.

Thank you to my literary agent, Ted Malawer, who saw potential in this book when it was just a glimmer of an idea and who helped it (and its author) grow in too many ways to name. Thank you as well to Chris Richman, Michael Stearns, and the whole Upstart Crow crew—I'm proud to be associated with you all.

The entire community of authors I've been lucky enough to be a part of has been wonderful to me and I'd thank you each individually if I could. Specifically, I'd like to give thanks to Shaun Hutchinson, who generously helped me brainstorm when I was stuck on an early draft of this book. To Suzanne Young, for encouragement and sage writerly advice such as "If you think it's funny, go for it!" which I have taken to mean "Add more ball jokes." And to Trish Doller, who is always there for me to bounce crazy ideas off.

And as always, thanks beyond thanks to my family: Mom, Dad, Julie, Matt, Kelly, and the kids. I love you.